Collars & Kittens

APRIL CROSS

LOVE IS IN THE AIR
SERIES

Don't let their small-town charm fool you—these men are anything but innocent.

When a radio show contest in a quaint town on the Oregon coast goes viral, women from all over the region are vying for a chance to win a date with one of the five sexy bachelors. But on Valentine's Day, when the chosen ladies arrive, they'll discover that real small-town men are way less vanilla than a movie fantasy. Will sparks fly and hearts be won, or will these arranged dates be a painful mess?

Contents

Dedicated to lovers of the soft doms who know how to masterfully turn up the heat where it matters most—in the bedroom.

Chapter 1

OLIVIA

My heart pounds as I pick up Agnes, my sweet, fluffy tabby cat. She's been lethargic since yesterday, and this morning she refused to eat. I'm frightened something is wrong with her, and I know I need to take her to a vet. I moved to Hazy Cove, Oregon a few weeks ago, and while I love this small town, I'm not sure where the closest vet is.

I grab my phone with a shaky hand and do an internet search. A clinic called "Paws and Claws" is only a couple of miles away. Shit, that's too far to walk.

Before moving here, I didn't have a car. My manipulative ex-fiancé, Ben, convinced me I shouldn't drive because I was accident prone, so I relied on public transportation when I lived in Seattle. I bought a used Corolla before the trip, and almost as soon as I drove into town, smoke started coming from under the hood. It's currently at the local mechanic.

If I didn't need to carry Agnes, I'd hoof it to the clinic, but I don't want her to be panicking for the thirty-minute walk. This sweet cat is the only family I have left after my mom died four years ago.

Hazy Cove might be small, but luckily, they have people working for a ride-sharing app most of the time, and I arrange for someone to pick us up. As I gently place Agnes in her carrier, she lets out a pitiful meow, and my heart hurts for her. I wish I could tell her she'll be okay, but she wouldn't understand. I coo softly to help soothe her, knowing we'll both feel better once the vet checks her over.

The sound of a car in the driveway alerts me that our ride has arrived. I take a deep breath to calm my nerves before heading out the door. The fresh ocean breeze rolls over me as soon as I step outside, the salty air crisp and invigorating—if a little chilly. But it doesn't settle the anxiety churning in my stomach. I clutch Agnes' carrier close, her soft meows plucking at my heartstrings.

The driver makes small talk on the way to the clinic, and I can tell he's trying to distract me from my worry. It helps, but I'm glad the ride isn't long. I haven't made any friends yet, and I've been a little lonely, so any chance I get to talk to someone brings out my rare extroverted side when I'm normally more reserved.

Even with the short time I've been here, leaving behind my toxic relationship with Ben feels like the best decision I've ever made. He doesn't know where I am. The only person from my former life who knows is my best friend Sierra, and there's no way in hell she'd tell him. Coming here was a clean break—one I desperately needed.

Hazy Cove is a small touristy town and is very welcoming. I feel like I'm quickly becoming a part of the community though I haven't made any close friends yet. The people living here genuinely care about each other, and there's a sense of camaraderie that I never experienced in Seattle.

I don't want to leave this town, and the idea of something bad happening to Agnes makes my anxiety level skyrocket. A bigger city would probably have better veterinarians if something is seriously wrong. I try to relax my muscles and focus on my breathing to calm down. Having a panic attack on the drive to the clinic won't help anything.

CHAPTER 2

OLIVIA

After getting trapped behind a car going ten miles per hour, we finally arrive at the clinic. I wasn't sure what to expect, but the clinic's exterior has a rustic charm with its weathered cedar shingles in a soft, silvery hue. The white trim and paw print sign above the entrance creates a cozy and welcoming scene.

A bell jingles when I walk in, and the air is infused with a pleasant lavender scent. A friendly older woman behind the desk welcomes me. "Hi there, you must be the new yoga teacher! How can I help you today?"

Yeah, everyone knows who I am even if I haven't met them yet. I hold up the carrier. "My cat, Agnes, isn't feeling well, and I'd like to see the vet as soon as possible."

The woman gives us a sympathetic smile and checks her computer. "Dr. Harrington can see our poor baby in about thirty minutes. Will that work?"

I nod, grateful that they can see Agnes so soon. "Yes, that would be wonderful. Thank you."

The woman's smile is radiant. "Great. Here's some paperwork to fill out, and make yourself comfortable. We've got water and snacks if you need anything."

She hands me a clipboard with a form on it, and I sit in the waiting room while I jot down Agnes' information. My sick kitty is twelve years old now, a rescue I adopted in high school. She's the most important creature in my life, especially after losing my mom. My father was killed in a motorcycle accident when I was a baby, so it was just me and my mom facing the world together for most of my life. The thought of possibly losing Agnes fills me with dread, and I refuse to contemplate it. The vet better be able to make her healthy again.

When I'm finished with the paperwork, I turn it in at the front desk with a polite smile, trying to hide my inner turmoil. The woman takes it from me and points to a door off to the side. "If you'd like to wait in the exam room, it's right through there. Dr. Harrington will be with you shortly."

I thank her and pick up the carrier. As I lug Agnes into the room, the antiseptic smell of cleaner greets me. The room is spotless, which instantly puts me more at ease. I'd never trust a clinic if the rooms were dirty.

There's a long metal table that I set the carrier on and open its door so Anges can crawl out and sniff around. She stares at me defiantly and doesn't move, so I sit in the chair next to the table, bouncing my leg as I try to be patient. Who is this Dr. Harrington? I imagine an old guy in his sixties who's living the quiet life in a coastal town, keeping the local pets healthy. The thought is oddly comforting. Surely he'll have years of experience.

As I wait for him to arrive, I listen to songs on a local radio station piped through speakers. The music isn't loud, and my mind wanders back to what brought me here: escaping the toxicity of my past relationship. Ben was controlling and manipulative, slowly isolating me from friends over the five years we were together until I only had Sierra left. Ben wanted me to be his successful trophy wife—a hotshot lawyer and arm candy for his political aspirations. He mentioned more than once that we'd be a power couple, as if that was the purpose of our relationship.

I don't know why I stayed with him for as long as I did, especially since he often hinted that my family being from Argentina helped me with school and in my career. As if I didn't earn my achievements through hard work and intellect. Yep, I should have dumped his ass as soon as he started undermining me like that.

Ben and I started fighting more, but I don't know what the final straw was. One morning I woke up and the fog in my brain had lifted. Every word out of Ben's mouth was condescending and controlling. I was just done. I wanted out, and something told me he'd try to make me stay, so I left a note that I was leaving. I haven't seen him since, and I'm happy to keep it that way.

I dropped out of law school, and Sierra helped me find an apartment for a couple of months, but I was living in fear of running into Ben anytime I went out. When Sierra had the idea that I could come to Hazy Cove and help her sister, Naomi, who owned the yoga studio and wanted to take maternity leave, it seemed like the ideal solution. I'd worked as a yoga instructor during college, so it didn't take long to certify as a trainer in Oregon.

Now my life is peaceful, and I'm finally able to be my true self—once I figure out who that is. I'm twenty-four years old, so I've still got time. The little cottage I rented is a few blocks from the beach, and I've decorated it in a way that makes me happy—rainbow colors and fluffy pillows. The best part about having my own place is that I was able to put my two stuffies on my couch. Ben always made fun of them, so they've been packed away in boxes for years, but as soon as I set out Glacia Pawsicle the polar bear and Shivers McFlap the penguin, it felt like home. Whenever I see them, it makes me happy and confirms I made the right decision to move to Oregon.

The door opens, snapping me to attention, and I stand up as a man looking down at a chart and wearing a white lab coat walks in. Okay, I was totally wrong about the vet being old. He's probably close to forty, tall and muscular, with a rugged, outdoorsy look. His wavy brown hair is tousled as if he ran his fingers through it, and a dusting of silver at his temples makes him appear distinguished and sexy. My fingers twitch, and I wonder if his hair is soft.

When he looks up from the chart and smiles in greeting, my mind goes blank and my body ignites with a scorching heat. The room fills with a woodsy scent from his cologne, and his eyes are a piercing sapphire that makes me feel like he can see down into the depths of my soul. I've never had this immediate of a visceral reaction to someone. My mouth goes dry as I shift my weight to my other foot nervously.

A flicker of amusement crosses his face, and my cheeks blaze with embarrassment and desire. Oh fuck, he knows he's having an effect on me. This just got awkward.

His voice is soothing and deep. "I'm Dr. Harrington. I hear you've got a sick kitty."

Right. Agnes. I'm here for my cat, not to ogle the dreamboat veterinarian. I try to respond calmly, as if meeting an insanely attractive man who stirs up unexpected desires is totally natural.

"Hi, Dr. Harrington. Yes, her name is Agnes."

Dr. Harrington gives me a warm smile, and I swear it's like he has an energy that envelops me, searing every brain cell I own and making it difficult to think straight.

"What seems to be the problem today?"

I giggle nervously, cursing myself for acting like a smitten schoolgirl. "Oh, um, her name is Olivia, and she's been lethargic the last two days, and this morning, she didn't eat."

"Olivia?" He raises an eyebrow, and his eyes twinkle. "Or is her name Agnes?"

My mouth pops open and then closes and then opens again, but nothing comes out. All the blood rushes to my face, which is now probably beet red. Shit. Why is he affecting me like this? I've encountered countless attractive men before, so why can't I keep it together long enough for my cat to receive treatment from this drop-dead gorgeous veterinarian? My mind scrambles for a response, but all I can do is stare at him, completely rattled.

I finally find my words again. "She's Agnes. *I'm* Olivia."

I glance over at Agnes, hoping the vet doesn't ask me to say anything else, because at the rate I'm going, I'll respond with something mortifying. Thankfully, Dr. Harrington chuckles, saving me from making a bigger fool out of myself.

"Poor kitty," he murmurs. "I'll take a look at her and see if I can get this sweet girl feeling better."

I watch as he unlatches the top of the carrier and gently pulls her out onto the table. She doesn't fight him—which is rare for her with strangers. She's usually afraid of anyone but me. My opinion of the doctor increases. I have complete faith that Agnes wouldn't trust a vet who was anything less than kind and competent.

Dr. Harrington spends several minutes checking her out, talking quietly and petting her. "Agnes, sweetheart, you're going to be fine."

He's talking to Agnes, but my brain hears his words as though he said them to me. The world is suddenly in slow motion, and all the stress melts from my body as his voice soothes me. Everything will be okay. He'll make her better.

While he's checking Agnes's ears, he asks conversationally, "So, what made you pick the name Agnes?"

I'm momentarily flustered by the question, my brain still addled by his presence, but I manage to respond. "Oh, she's from a shelter, and that was the name on her paperwork. I didn't want her to have to learn a new name, along with adjusting to a new life, so I kept it."

Ben always thought my reasoning was stupidly sentimental, but I swear Agnes knows her name. I wasn't going to take that small bit of familiarity from her after she was abandoned. That would've been cruel.

While Dr. Harrington stays focused on examining Agnes, I'm able to openly admire him. He's got large, capable hands—with no wedding ring—and he's being so gentle. Her purr is loud in the tiny room, as if she's enjoying the attention. Yeah, I'd probably love those hands massaging me, too. I bet he could make me purr.

Fuck, I shouldn't be thinking this way. Isn't it wrong to objectify someone sexually, no matter how attractive they are? And he's way too old for me anyway. I need to get my mind out of the gutter and remember why I'm here.

When he finishes and stares at me expectantly, I realize he must have asked a question while I was daydreaming about those talented hands roaming my body. Whoops.

"Sorry, what did you say?"

He doesn't answer for a moment, and the intensity of his blue eyes pulls at something deep in my core. Our gazes lock, and I can feel my entire body responding to him again as my heart races and my skin tingles. It's pretty inconvenient to be lusting after my cat's vet, but there's something about him that stirs up desires I haven't felt in months—probably me and every other hot-blooded woman in this town. I swear the air is charged with sexual energy, but it's probably wishful thinking. It's been way too long since I've had sex. I make a mental note to dig out my sex toys as soon as I get home.

After I broke up with Ben, it took me a couple of months to figure out what I was doing with my life, and I haven't been interested in playing with my sex toys. Hell, Ben was my first and only lover, and Dr. Harrington is the first guy I've been attracted to since becoming single. I'm not used to this feeling. My libido is coming out of hibernation, but did it have to be today?

I need to pull myself together. I'm acting like a romance novel character making eyes at the sexy small-town veterinarian—well, with my kinky self as the protagonist, it would have to be an erotica...but that's not the point. He's not going to bend me over this exam table, no matter how much I wish he would. Those things don't happen outside of books.

After a pause that feels endless, he gives Agnes a gentle scratch behind her ears and repeats himself in that deep voice. "She's a little dehydrated, which would make her not feel great, so I'd like to give her some fluids under the skin. I can also do some blood work to rule out any other issues."

I let out a sigh of relief, grateful he knows what he's doing. "Okay. That sounds good."

He nods, all business again. "I'll just step out for a few minutes with Anges and fix her right up."

After he leaves with Agnes, I sink back into the chair, feeling flushed. Grabbing a magazine with horses on the cover, I fan myself with it. I need to pull it together before he returns. I'm sure he's got women falling at his feet all the time. A mature, successful man like him probably has a line of eager dates. And here I am, a mess over a simple vet visit.

When the door opens, I casually drop the magazine back in the rack, trying to look nonchalant. Agnes has a little bandage on her leg where he drew blood, and she clearly isn't happy about it. My heart goes out to her. Poor baby.

"All done. Agnes was very brave," Dr. Harrington says gently as he sets her back on the table. Agnes gives him an indignant glare, and I have to stifle a laugh.

He nods, gently stroking Agnes's back in a way that makes me envious. "It's always scary when our fur babies are under the weather. But Agnes seems like a real fighter."

His words are reassuring and professional, dispelling some of the charged tension. Everything is over quickly after that. He returns Agnes to her carrier and brings her out to the lobby, with me following.

"Once you pay at the desk, I'll take her out to your car for you," he offers.

That makes me laugh weakly. "Oh, no need. I have to call for a ride. My car is in the shop."

He glances at the clock on the wall. "Well, it's around lunchtime. I can give you a lift home if you'd like. I was going to pick up a package at the post office anyway." He turns to the woman at the front desk. "Sue, you'll lock up when you go to lunch, right?"

Sue beams. "Of course, Dr. Harrington. You two go right ahead."

He didn't exactly ask if I wanted a ride, just assumed, but I'm not going to turn down a free trip. And, if I'm being honest, the idea of being close to him in the confined space of a car is far too appealing.

"Thank you so much. I really appreciate it," I say, hoping I don't sound overeager.

He gives me a grin that makes my toes curl. "Happy to help. Shall we?"

I quickly pay the bill, hyper aware of his presence beside me as the clean, woodsy scent of him envelops me. Before I can think better of it, I'm saying, "Ready when you are."

Well, at least I'll have a few more minutes to admire him. He switches his lab coat for a jacket, and as we walk out to his SUV, I wrack my brain for something normal to chat about. I want to give him a better impression of me, and I'm running out of time. "So, do you enjoy being a small-town vet?"

Dr. Harrington smiles over at me as he opens the back door to settle Agnes in. "Yes, I really do. The community here is great."

We slide into the front seats, and the leather creaks softly beneath us. I give him directions to my little cottage as we pull out of the parking lot. Now that we're in the vehicle, I try not to stare at him and watch the passing town as he talks. It's not even the middle of January, and some of the businesses are already gearing up for Valentine's Day.

"I actually grew up in Colorado," Dr. Harrington continues. "My neighbors were both vets, and I looked up to them so much. I think that planted the seed early on that this is what I wanted to do."

"That's really sweet," I say with genuine interest, turning back to him and picturing him as a younger, animal-loving version of himself.

As we chat, he tells me his parents are retired and still living in Colorado. His eyes are mostly on the road, but he keeps stealing glances at me. Is he checking me out? Nah, I doubt it.

All too soon, we pull into my driveway. He insists on helping me take the carrier inside despite my protests.

"It's no trouble at all," he assures me with a smile. "Agnes is lucky to have a doting owner."

When we step into my living room, I reach for the carrier handle, suddenly shy. "Thank you again for everything."

He hesitates, holding my gaze. "Of course. Let me know if you need anything else." His voice drops lower on the last words. "Anything at all."

Heat floods my cheeks at his meaningful tone. Is he saying...? No, I'm imagining things.

"I will. T-thanks again," I stammer out.

I set Anges' carrier on the floor while he pulls a business card from his wallet with deft fingers. "Call me if she gets worse, but she should be fine. The results will take two to three days, and I'll let you know once I have them."

Our fingers brush as I take the card, sending a current of energy through me, and his eyes widen slightly. Did he feel that too?

For a long moment we stand there, the air thick with sexual chemistry. I get lost in the depths of his gaze, the rest of the world falling away. I wish he would touch me.

Agnes's indignant yowl breaks the spell, and we step apart quickly.

"I should let her out," I say with an embarrassed laugh. "Thank you again, Dr. Harrington, for everything."

He laughs, the sound rich and warm. "I'm glad I could help, and please, call me Dalton. It's not often I get to enjoy a car ride with such a good kitty."

When he says 'good kitty,' a thought pops into my head—I could be his kitty. I'd do whatever he wanted if he called me a good girl with that deep voice of his.

Before he turns to leave, he glances at my couch, and his eyes linger on Glacia Pawsicle and Shivers McFlap before murmuring, "Take care, Olivia. You know where to find me if you need me."

I have a sudden flash of all the different ways I could need him...how about showing me that not all men are assholes? My ex who never treated me like anything but a submissive who was there to service his needs in bed. Ben never once went down on me, and I bet an older man knows what he's doing down there.

Holy fuck, I need to clear my head. Everything out of Dalton's mouth sounds so sexy, but I know he didn't mean his words the way I'm taking them. I can feel my panties growing damp, and I desperately need to get away from him. "Yes, sir—Dalton—thanks again for everything."

His eyes flicker to mine again briefly before he walks back to his SUV. My heart pounds as I give him a little wave. What just happened? Was that all in my imagination? Thank God he didn't laugh at my stuffies.

I let Agnes out of the carrier, and she immediately headbutts my hand, demanding attention. I stroke her soft fur absently, still distracted by thoughts of Dr. Harrington...no, Dalton, I correct myself.

It's ridiculous, I barely know the man. Not to mention he's clearly too old for me. What would a mature, established guy like him want with a twenty-four-year-old yoga instructor who's just getting back on her feet after a toxic relationship?

And yet...there was an undeniable connection between us. A zing of attraction. Ugh, it doesn't matter. It's not like anything will come of it. He was just being friendly.

After a few minutes of petting her, Agnes loses interest and saunters off happily to her favorite sunny patch on the living room rug. I envy her ability to live in the moment.

Now, all I have to do is wait to hear from Dalton.

I wish it wasn't going to be a conversation about my cat. A girl can dream, can't she?

With a sigh, I try in vain to redirect my thoughts to anything but the magnetic pull I felt toward this near stranger. Easier said than done.

Chapter 3

DALTON

I've designed my clinic to be warm and inviting. The walls are painted a tranquil shade of blue, reminiscent of a clear sky. In the lobby, comfortable armchairs circle a rustic coffee table stacked with pet magazines. A muted aromatherapy scent wafts through the air, masking the inevitable smells that come with animals and the cleaners we use. My goal is to create a peaceful oasis, easing the nerves of the anxious pets and owners.

As the sole vet in our small town, the clinic is my second home. I live in the apartment upstairs, remaining on call at all hours. When I'm in the clinic, my door stays open—I want Sue at the front desk and my part-time tech to know I'm available if they need me. I love my job, exhausting as it can be. The long hours and demanding work are worth it to care for the creatures who bring such joy to our lives.

After yesterday's encounter, today is boring in comparison. I can't stop thinking about Olivia. She was stunning, with a slight frame, warm beige skin, and beautiful brown eyes with golden flecks. Normally, I assume a woman that gorgeous knows the effect she has on people, but she also had this endearing awkwardness that made me want to keep her safe from all the bad things in the world—and fuck me, that adorable blush when she called me 'sir'...it's been months since I've gotten aroused so quickly.

Of course, she's far too young for the likes of me. Not that it stops my thoughts from wandering where they shouldn't. Fantasizing about fucking her cute little mouth, watching those plump lips stretch around me...but some things simply aren't meant to be. I'm not looking for a one-night stand with a young hottie.

I ready my supplies to see my first patient of the day, eager for the distraction. The radio plays softly in the background, chatter from the local station drifting through the office. It's always on in the clinic, a sense of connection to our small town. I find myself tapping along to the songs as I work.

With Valentine's Day approaching, love is in the air—at least according to the radio hosts. Local businesses are running themed promotions, and the stores are festooned with pink and red. Despite my general disinterest in holidays, their enthusiasm is contagious. It's hard not to get caught up in the festivities.

As I examine a golden retriever with an irritated ear, I overhear the DJs announcing a Valentine's Day contest. They're seeking local bachelors who are willing to take a chance on love. Once the contest starts, women will submit applications to win a date with one of the guys. Interesting approach to finding a partner, though not something I'd consider.

I try to imagining who might participate. The guys from the motorcycle shop seem likely, with their bold attitudes. Our straight-laced high school coach, Mike? Doubtful. Too proper for something so unpredictable. Plenty of single men in our BDSM circle, but slim pickings for partners with compatible kinks in a small town.

The idea of entering the contest sticks with me. What if I used the platform to promote animal welfare this winter? Educational outreach, despite my disinterest in dating. After all, saving one pet would make it worthwhile...

Plus, my exes always said I had a voice made for sexy audios and asked me to make them a recording where I called them a dirty little slut and told them how much of a good girl they were. I have a deep, resonant voice that draws people in. Maybe it'll give me an edge with a radio show contest.

The retriever is treated, his owner is delighted, and they are on their way. Once I'm alone, I make up my mind. I'm going to give the contest a shot. What do I have to lose? Submitting an application can't hurt.

During a lull at work, I complete the application on the station's website. They want basic information from me, such as my age, job, and philosophy about life. I try to showcase my humor and passion for animals. The final thing they want is a question they can ask my potential dates. Easy enough—I want to know what pets the woman has. Before I can overthink it, I hit submit. It's official now—I'm in the running, if they pick me.

After applying, I phone my best friend, Travis, in the next town over. We chat at least weekly, and I'd rather tell him myself that I entered rather than have him hear it from someone else. He loves that radio station—he'll be tickled I entered their contest.

He answers in his usual teasing tone. "Let me guess, calling about the cheesy dating contest they announced on the radio?"

I laugh loudly. Of course he already knows. Not much happens in our small towns without Travis hearing about it. "I figured you already submitted your application," I volley back.

"Ha! No way, but I was curious if you were going to."

"That's actually why I called. I applied this morning."

"No shit?" He sounds skeptical. "You, Mr. Hermit Vet, entered a dating contest?"

"Hey, I'm not a hermit. But yes, I figured it was a chance to promote animal welfare. I'll use the spotlight for some public outreach."

Travis doesn't sound convinced. "Uh huh. That's the only reason, I'm sure."

"It is. I can't think of any women in town I want to date."

Well, except for Olivia, a traitorous part of my mind reminds me, but she's too young, despite my attraction to her.

"Maybe not long term, but you could have a little fun," Travis suggests slyly. "Like that curvy cupcake baker, she's sexy."

I nearly choke. He doesn't know I've considered asking Maddie out before. "Nah, she's too sweet for a guy like me."

"Like she knows how kinky you really are. I bet she imagines cuddling all night with the softie vet with the dreamy voice."

I laugh more loudly. He doesn't know how close that is to the truth. I was much kinkier in my twenties, but I'm getting softer as I age.

Travis and I joke around a bit more about how I don't need the pet owners wondering about my sex life while I'm saving the lives of their pets before we hang up.

As unlikely as it seems I'll meet anyone I click with, the thought of a woman seeing the real me, not the professional vet side, ignites a spark of hope inside me. I married too young and divorced before I was 30, and I've learned a lot about myself since then—enough to know that any future relationship I have needs better communication than my marriage.

My ex-wife, Misty, wanted a total power exchange relationship where I was always the dom, and I tried to be her everything. It took me way too long to admit it wasn't working for me, that isn't who I am. By the time we finally talked about it, too many resentments had built up, and she wasn't willing to compromise.

Since my divorce, I've tried online dating, but I'm afraid of falling back into old habits of being a dom too often. I'm happy to spank a woman's ass red in the bedroom, but that's not the sum of who I am. I need someone who enjoys quiet nights of snuggling on the couch and watching movies just as much as she likes my hard dom side.

The real issue is that I'm set in my ways, and I don't need to date. The local kink community might be small, but within the neighboring towns, I'm able to find play partners if I need to blow off steam. I'd have to love someone to disrupt my comfortable life. The chances of finding that special person on a radio show dating contest are slim to none, so it's good I'm only planning on using the opportunity to talk about pets if I'm chosen.

Well, nothing to do but wait and see what happens. I push away thoughts of Olivia's blushing face, how she called me sir...

No use dwelling on impossibilities. I turn my focus back to my furbaby patients, determined not to get ahead of myself.

CHAPTER 4

OLIVIA

I curl up on the couch with my laptop, a steaming mug of tea, and a purring Agnes, who's feeling much better after her trip to the vet a few weeks ago. It's an enormous relief that nothing was seriously wrong with her.

When Dalton called with the blood test results, he was annoyingly professional, sticking to the facts about her health. He suggested I switch her to a senior formula cat food and watch her closely to make sure she's drinking enough. I bought her a fountain that's supposed to entice kitties to drink more water. I was worried Anges wouldn't like it, but she took to it right away, and from how often I have to refill it, I can tell she's drinking more.

I lean into the soft cushions and take a sip of my tea before calling Sierra to video chat. It's weird living so far away from her now, but we're staying in close contact weekly to gossip and catch up.

Sierra answers, her face filling my screen. "Livvy! Oh my God, I feel like I haven't talked to you in forever!"

Seeing her excitement makes me grin. "I know, it's been a whole six days! How are you? How's life in Seattle?"

Sierra launches into a detailed account of her latest date, a new job prospect, and the ins and outs of her book club drama. I laugh at her stories, feeling like I'm right there with her.

After forty minutes of nonstop chatter, she finally slows down. "Okay, enough about me. What's new with you? Any hot yoga students I need to know about?" She wiggles her eyebrows suggestively.

"Oh yes, so many hot yoga students. I'm swimming in male attention." My tone is sarcastic. Sierra knows that most of my yoga students are women who are middle aged or older.

She sticks out her tongue. "You know what I mean. When are you going to start dating again?"

I shrug, sobering a bit. "I don't know. After everything with Ben, I'm not sure I'm ready."

"I get that, I do." Sierra gives me a sympathetic look through the screen. "But you deserve to find someone who treats you right. Someone who makes you happy."

"Maybe someday."

We're both quiet for a moment as years of friendship pass between us before her eyes twinkle mischievously. "Well, until Mr. Right comes along, I have something that might interest you."

"Oh? Do tell."

She grins. "Have you heard of the KHZY Hazy Cove Radio Valentine's Day contest?"

My curiosity is piqued. "No, what's that?"

"They've got a bunch of eligible bachelors in your town who are offering themselves up for a date on Valentine's Day. You have to apply on their website."

I snort. "You know I don't like dating websites."

Am I ready to date again? I keep the thought to myself because I'm not sure of the answer.

She rolls her eyes. "Livvy, this is how people meet these days. But this isn't a dating website, it's a contest. You don't have a guy in your life, so what's the harm in looking?"

I giggle nervously as my stomach tightens into knots. "I don't know."

I'm not willing to admit how afraid I am to date after what happened with Ben. The breakup shattered my self-confidence, and I don't know who I am anymore. I'm happier, but I'm like a different person from the one who thought she was going to be a lawyer. I used to think I was in charge of my life and knew exactly what I wanted. Now I second guess myself on everything, and I don't like it. Just...how did Ben fool me for so long? Why didn't I see he was a jackass?

"Come on, Olivia. Don't overthink it."

Sierra can tell I'm not seriously considering it, and after she needles me for twenty minutes, I finally give in. "All right, all right. I'll look at it. But I'm not promising anything."

She grins. "That's all I ask, darling. I want you to have some fun. And who knows? Maybe you'll find a smoking-hot firefighter on the list."

An image of Dr. Dalton Harrington pops into my head. How about a smoking-hot veterinarian instead? There's no way he'd be in the contest, that's a pipe dream.

"Let me know if you see any hotties. I expect full reports."

I laugh, shaking my head. "You got it. I'll give you all the steamy details."

We chat for a few more minutes before reluctantly saying goodnight. I love connecting with Sierra. It makes me feel less alone.

After we hang up, I glance at the clock. It's getting late, but I'm not quite ready for bed yet. I pull up the contest website Sierra mentioned, figuring I'll take a quick peek.

The KHZY website is professional, better than I expected, and the contest link is easy to find. There are photos and short bios for five local men. I scroll through curiously, recognizing a couple I saw around town. Most are decent guys, but no one catches my—

I freeze, doing a double take. Dr. Dalton Harrington's handsome face smiles up at me from the screen. Holy shit. He actually entered this thing?

His bio says he's the only vet in Hazy Cove—I snicker at that. As if this town is big enough for more than one—and he's never done anything like this before. If he had one wish, he's hoping to promote animal welfare while spending an enjoyable evening with a local woman. Aww, what a sweetheart.

As I read about the contest and the rules and skim over information about radio interviews before and after the date, I'm intrigued and can't help but imagine what it might be like to go on a date with Dalton. Would he be a gentleman, or does he have a fiery side?

The website says that I can submit a dating request for the specific man I'm interested in by filling out a questionnaire. After February 7th, the men will look through the women and choose their winners. It's not like Dalton would actually choose me, so I'm not sure why I'm considering trying.

My thoughts race as images and fantasies of what I want him to do to me play in a continuous loop, each more vivid and tantalizing than the last. I can feel my panties growing damp as I debate whether I should enter. This is a crazy idea, right? He's way too old for me, but more importantly, I'm not ready to date. It would be wrong to win when I have no intention of anything long term...but God, he's so damn sexy.

I think back, picturing his massive hands, and a shiver runs down my body. After Agnes's appointment, I unpacked my sex toys and spent some time reconnecting with my sexuality. I almost forgot how nice it is to do something for my own pleasure. I can thank Dalton for waking up that part of myself again.

Since then, I've been playing with my toys regularly and daydreaming about a real cock inside me or finally finding out what the big deal is about a guy going down on you. Half of the time, that imaginary cock is connected to someone who looks suspiciously like Dalton. Why keep playing with my toys when I have the chance of getting the real thing? It's just one date, it's not like we're walking down the aisle to the altar.

Before I can talk myself out of it, I start the application. If I miraculously won, it would be one night. A fun way to dip my toe back into dating without too much pressure. I upload a recent photo of myself and fill out my basic information.

Name: Olivia Ruiz.

Age: 24.

Occupation: Part-time yoga instructor, full-time cat mom.

Despite the low odds of being selected, I feel a little giddy as I fill out the rest of the form. I add in some flirty comments about how Agnes and I need some excitement in our lives. The last question gives me pause.

Question: Share a list of your household pets, their names, and what they mean to you.

This one had to be something Dalton wrote in since it's not really a question. At first glance, the request is boring. Yet, the invitation to discuss 'what they mean to me' subtly hints that he's hunting for an animal lover. He's already met Agnes, so talking about her wouldn't be memorable. I need to dazzle him.

I tap my fingertips on the edge of my laptop while I contemplate how to answer. When a brilliant idea tickles my fancy, I giggle and spend twenty minutes rewriting it at least four times before I'm satisfied.

I reread my answer and laugh. There's nothing subtle about what I wrote, but at least he won't think I'm looking to marry him. There's a tiny part of me that's terrified I'll actually win, but the more rational part of me tells that other part to shut up and let myself have some fun again.

My finger hovers over the submit button, hesitating for just a moment before decisively pressing down. There. Done.

I close my laptop, feeling accomplished. The idea of a date with Dalton is appealing, especially if I wasn't imagining our connection. Even if he doesn't select me, at least I put myself out there. It's progress.

The next morning, I see the contest has blown up on social media overnight and news outlets all the way up to Seattle are splashing around articles about the sexy bachelors looking for dates. As I walk to the yoga studio for my morning class, I stew over all the posts and articles I read. Well, there goes my chance.

By the time I arrive at the studio, I'm a tense ball of nerves. Once class starts, I take my place in front of everyone and try to center myself. One deep breath in, long exhale out.

"Welcome, everyone. Let's begin with a few gentle stretches."

I lead my students through a series of poses, sounding calm and collected. With each flowing pose, I feel my anxiety start to dissipate.

I move gracefully through the positions, my body bending and arching with practiced ease. The familiar rituals soothe me, reminding me I'm exactly where I want to be, and that I don't need a date with Dalton to be happy.

After class, I tidy up the studio, feeling more relaxed. As I walk to my car that I finally got back from the shop, I decide to treat myself to a vanilla latte from the cafe down the street. The February air is crisp but sunny—excellent for sitting outside with my warm drink and soaking up the vitamin D that's hard to get enough of in Oregon.

Coffee in hand, I head toward the patio seating outside the cafe. Rounding the corner, I nearly collide with a broad chest. Strong hands grasp my shoulders, steadying me. I look up into a pair of sapphire-blue eyes.

"Whoa there," Dalton says with a crooked smile. "Careful."

My heart skips a beat at his touch. I take a small step back, hoping the immediate flush in my cheeks isn't too obvious.

"Dalton, hi!" I try to sound casual. I'm assuming he has no idea I entered the contest last night.

His voice is warm and gravelly. "Getting your caffeine fix?"

I hold up my latte sheepishly. "Yeah, just what I need this morning. You?"

He lifts his own to-go cup. "Same here. Afternoon appointments at the clinic. Gotta stay fueled up."

I nod, hyper aware of how close we're standing on the small patio. "Makes sense. Busy day ahead?"

"The usual," he says, glancing at his phone, and smiles apologetically at me. "In fact, I should probably get going."

"Of course, don't let me keep you." I shift my weight, reluctant for our interaction to end but unsure of what else to say.

He hesitates, looking at me like he wants to say something, but all he comes out with is, "All right, I have to run. See you around, Olivia."

With a wave, he turns and strides off down the street. I stand frozen for a moment, heart pounding, watching his retreating figure. That man is going to be the death of me. But what a way to go.

I find an empty table on the patio and sit down to enjoy my drink, replaying our conversation in my head while I buzz with giddy energy. At least now he'll remember me when he sees my entry for a date with him.

God, I hope he chooses me.

CHAPTER 5

DALTON

It's after hours at my practice, and I need some privacy to go through the applications sent over by the radio show. I was surprised yet pleased when they contacted me to tell me I was one of the chosen bachelors, and I've been waiting for the information on the women who want a date with me.

Since I'm not looking for a love match, I'm more interested in finding someone who will be a fun dinner companion—someone I have something in common with to avoid any uncomfortable conversation.

I light a eucalyptus and mint candle on the side table before sinking into the worn-out leather chair in front of my screen. It's time to pick the person for my Valentine's date, and the scents should help me focus. As I work through the applications, I find that most of the answers feel generic, like the women are telling me what they think I want to hear. I'm also taken aback by how many applicants aren't from Oregon. Since the contest went viral, there are women from Seattle all the way down to Los Angeles trying to score a date. Don't get me wrong, I know I clean up nice enough, but I'm no celebrity bachelor.

I chuckle as I come across a couple of women making straight up offers to let me pet their pussies. I really should have seen that one coming. Travis is going to find that funny when I tell him.

About halfway in, I'm starting to lose hope of finding someone I feel a connection with. I roll my shoulders back to stretch as I click over to the next application. When the photo appears, I freeze.

Well, hello there, Olivia Ruiz.

My pulse speeds up as I take in her big brown eyes and long dark hair. I haven't been able to stop thinking about her since we met that day at my clinic. The way she called me "sir" and could barely string two sentences together around me. There's something spellbinding about her combination of innocence and allure that's haunted me ever since.

Bumping into her at the coffee shop didn't help. The way her yoga pants hugged her curves...I'm a sucker for a woman in yoga pants, and they highlighted her fabulous legs. She's gorgeous, but there's no way I could date her. There's a wholesome quality about her that I don't want to corrupt with my perverted old self.

I scan down her application, noting that she's twenty-four—ouch. Okay, I knew she was young, but fifteen years younger is too much of an age difference for me. She's a part-time yoga instructor and full-time cat mom...which means she'd be in yoga pants. Often. I suddenly feel like the universe is fucking with me.

The two times I met her, she seemed tongue-tied and shy, but her answers to the questions are charming and articulate. I'm fascinated by the difference.

When I get to my request to know about her pets, I read through her answer slowly.

`You're asking the wrong question.`

I am? What's the right question?

`The real question we should explore is what makes me uniquely captivating.`

Oh, Olivia. I'm already captivated. You don't have to convince me.

`Allow me to highlight that I possess an extraordinary level of flexibility, courtesy of my devotion to yoga.`

All thoughts drain from my head as I imagine her in those sexy, tight yoga pants and in a downward dog pose. Well, she succeeded in putting filthy thoughts into my head.

But why stop there? Let's add a dash of whimsy—imagine a penchant for pink, sparkly collars that proudly proclaim 'kitten'.

I do a double take and read the sentence again. Is she telling me she likes BDSM pet play, or is this a collar for Agnes? There's one last line.

And, for the cherry on top, I offer a playful admission: I can be delightfully obedient when the situation demands it.

A vivid image pops into my mind of her on her knees, a pink collar around her slender neck, gazing up at me with those big doe eyes.

Oh yeah, I'm fucked.

I shift in my seat as my pants grow tighter. Down boy, I scold myself. I can't deny I'm interested. The Olivia here is bolder, more playful than the bashful woman I met before. I need to know her better.

Before I can overthink it, I email the radio station that Olivia is my choice. This is just a friendly dinner. I can rein in my baser impulses for one night. One little date with the charming Ms. Ruiz can't hurt, and then I can find out which Olivia is the real Olivia—the temptress in her application, or the charming sweetheart I met in person.

What will I do if she's the temptress?

I shake my head to clear it and pick up my phone to call Travis. He'll want to know who I selected, so I might as well get the teasing over with.

"Hey Doc, what's shaking?"

I smile. "I picked my date for the radio contest."

"Oooh, let me guess. You chose the one offering to let you pet her pussy?"

I snort. Is that the first thing everyone thinks? "Give me some credit, man. I chose someone I actually want to have a conversation with."

"Uh huh, sure. So who's the lucky lady?"

"First, you have to promise not to tell anyone. I think I'm not supposed to reveal my choice until the radio show announces it."

Travis lets out a huff. "As if I'd tell anyone. Now spill it."

How do I explain this? "Well, she's a bit younger than me."

"How young are we talking?" I can hear the grin in his voice.

"She's twenty-four."

He whistles. "Damn, going for a hot young thing, eh? You must be getting tired of ol' Faithful Rosie Palms."

I roll my eyes, already regretting telling him. I should have made him wait to hear it with everyone else. "Don't be crass. She's perfectly nice."

And perfectly delicious in those yoga pants.

His lowers his voice, as if he's telling me a secret. "You know, younger women are hella kinky these days. It might be time to dust off the old Dom suit and put the studded cockring on."

Yep, I should have kept quiet. "You have such a one-track mind. This is a dinner date, nothing more."

"Mmm hmm, suuure," he drags out. "You've been single for far too long. This might be good for you."

I bristle slightly. "I date occasionally. I'm just...careful after my disaster of a marriage."

"I get it man, but it's been more than 10 years since your divorce. Dating someone else might be exactly what you need. You can't let one bad apple ruin the bunch."

I inwardly groan at his metaphor. Still, he has a point. Since my divorce, I've kept things light, no real commitments. Maybe I have been guarding myself too much. We chat a few more minutes before hanging up.

I picture sitting across from Olivia at a restaurant, gazing into those endless brown eyes, making her smile...I shake my head, laughing softly at myself. Look at me, acting like a teenager with a crush. It's a friendly dinner date, I remind myself again. One pleasant evening getting to know Ms. Olivia Ruiz.

So why do I suddenly feel like I'm standing on the edge of something bigger? That spending more time with this beguiling woman might lead me somewhere I never expected? Shit, I need to stop making this more than it is.

I turn off the lights and head to bed. As I close my eyes, a vision of Olivia wearing a pink collar, performing a supple yoga bend, makes it difficult to fall asleep.

Well, damn. Maybe Travis is right. I have a feeling this date with Olivia is going to be anything but simple. My last thought before I fall asleep is that I better bring some condoms with me on the date...just in case.

Chapter 6

OLIVIA

As I sit on the couch with my laptop on my knees, an email pops up from the radio station—Dalton chose me for his Valentine's Day date. My heart races at an alarming pace. Unable to contain my excitement, I slam my laptop onto the coffee table and fling myself onto the couch cushions face first, muffling a high-pitched squeal. I grab Shivers McFlap and press a kiss to his beak, feeling a rush of excitement overwhelm me. I roll onto my side and squeeze the stuffie tightly in a hug. Oh my God, Dalton picked me!

After calming myself down, I email the radio station back to confirm, and then I spend the rest of the day pacing around my apartment with the jitters. There are so many things I need to do before this date. I need to get a mani/pedi and waxed. Shit, I need to go to one of the neighboring towns for that. There's no way in hell I want it circulating through Hazy Cove that the new yoga instructor got a Brazilian before her date with the sexy veterinarian...people would talk. I'll book an appointment at a spa in Ditzel Springs.

There are two adorable grandmas in my yoga class, Wanda and Daisy, and listening to them together tells me that the gossip mill is alive and well in Hazy Cove. I'm probably going to be grilled heavily about the date during the first class after Valentine's Day.

As much as the thought of the entire town talking about my date is nerve-wracking, knowing I'm going out with Dalton is thrilling. I hope he chose me because I said I can be obedient. Once I decided I needed some no-strings-attached sex, it was all I could think about, and now

I'm having vivid daydreams about submitting to Dalton. It's hard to explain to people who aren't subs, but I could tell Dalton was a dom, and something inside me knows he can give me exactly what I'm craving.

When I wake up on Valentine's Day, there's a dull throbbing sensation between my thighs, and the remnant of an erotic dream flashes through my mind. Dalton had me bent over an exam table in his clinic and was fucking me while he praised me for being a good little slut. I really want that, but I'm uncertain what to expect tonight. I mean, I doubt he'll fuck me over an exam table, so I need to stop daydreaming about it. I'm desperate enough that anything sounds delightful.

There was a required interview before the date, and we had the option to be on air together, but knowing how hard it is for me to talk coherently around Dalton, I told the radio show I wanted to do my interview alone. The only communication I've had with Dalton has been through the radio show, informing me that he'll be here at 6 p.m. to pick me up.

Did he choose me because I made it clear I was an easy lay, or was there another reason? I'd like to think he's attracted to me beyond my slutty response to his question, but since I want us to end up in bed, does it matter? I'm considering him a rebound fuck, and I need to get him out of my system so I can stop obsessing about him.

As I savor my morning tea, my mind replays the on-air interview I did with the radio show. The DJs, Delilah and James, were delightful to talk to, and they did a great job of keeping the ball rolling. We talked about how I met Dalton when my cat was sick, and they joked that it was love at first sight. I know they were playing it up for the listeners. I hope I came off as buoyant and self-assured, not some giddy schoolgirl. Being in the public eye doesn't come naturally to me, and the woman who entered the contest was fearless and playful. I'm able to pretend I'm that person for a short time, and I'm proud of myself for not tripping all over my words. I doubt anyone could tell I was shaking in my boots on the inside.

Dalton's solo interview on the radio station made me want to fuck him just for his voice. God, I could just imagine him whispering dirty talk in my ear while he pulls my hair and pounds into me. That guy could say anything, and I'd want to listen to him all night long. I don't remember too much of what he said in the interview since I spent most of the time daydreaming about fucking him.

The caffeine finally wakes me up, and as I watch Agnes nibble on her food, I can feel my anxiety building. There's a huge disconnect between the woman I am now and the woman I used to be before my breakup, and I'm afraid of making a horrible choice again. How can I ever trust myself to know a good guy from a bad one after what happened with Ben? What if Dalton is an asshole who wants to fuck a twenty-four-year-old and he doesn't care about my pleasure? He could be another Ben in disguise for all I know.

Wait, what if Dalton doesn't actually want to fuck me? I'm being a little presumptuous here.

Jesus, this damn date tonight has me in a tailspin. One minute I'm excited and euphoric, and the next I'm freaking out. Maybe I shouldn't have entered the contest, but my brain was overcome with lust. All I could think about was getting Dalton in bed. I never thought about what would happen if he rejects me—the embarrassment and humiliation of that. Ugh.

When my phone vibrates on the counter, I glance at the screen to see Sierra's name flash across the front. Of course she'd call now.

I pick up the phone. "Good morning!"

I'm aiming for cheery but fall short of the mark.

She answers me in her usual bubbly tone. "Hi there! Are you excited about your big date?"

Ugh. Why did I enter the contest? How did I convince myself this was a smart idea?

"Yeah," I mutter half-heartedly. "I can't wait."

"Uh oh, what's the matter?"

Sierra sounds concerned. Damn her and her sixth sense about me.

"It's…" I pause, debating how honest I should be. "What if he's not interested?"

"Liv, seriously. If you're having second thoughts about dating again, then cancel. No one is forcing you to go tonight."

Sierra is great for calling me on my bullshit. She's the bestest friend a girl could ask for, but damn it, she doesn't have to be so insightful all the time.

"You're right," I grumble, wishing she wasn't.

"Of course I'm right," she chirps brightly. "Now, tell me what you're wearing tonight."

God, she knows me too well. I run down my plans for my outfit, and after chatting with her for a while, I feel a little calmer. Tonight isn't a big deal. I'm going to have fun, and who cares what happens afterwards?

To prepare for the date, I take a long, indulgent bath, letting the hot water and the scent of a lavender bath bomb soothe away any lingering anxiety. I emerge feeling refreshed.

The afternoon passes quickly, and when it's time to get ready, I'm surprised to find my excitement and desire have returned after my doubts earlier.

The dress I plan to wear is a short pink number that's both elegant and alluring. I want to appear interested but not too eager—let's pretend my slutty answer in the application never happened—and I can't resist the chance to flaunt my legs, my best asset.

Realizing I only have 30 minutes before he's due to pick me up, I hurriedly slip on my pink lace bra and panty set. I'm feeling sexy and more confident with every piece of clothing I put on. When my hair and makeup are flawless, I slide on a pair of strappy high heels—another nod to my best feature because they make my calves look stellar. The last ritual is a spritz of my favorite vanilla-scented perfume. I'm ready.

The doorbell rings, and my heart pounds as I open it. Dalton stands in front of the door, and his broad shoulders and chiseled jawline make my body sing. Mmm, I want him. His dark hair is perfectly styled, and his blue eyes shine with excitement. His outfit is casual yet stylish—fitted jeans and a gray polo shirt that's unbuttoned at the top.

A small smile plays on his lips, and he's holding a stuffie of a white owl in one hand. I freeze in shock, and my heart melts. I can't lift my eyes from the stuffed animal. What am I going to name it?

"Hello, Olivia," he says, his voice resonating with a warmth that makes me quiver in delight.

All of a sudden, I remember where we are and that it must seem like an eternity since I opened the door.

I blink at him. "Hey, you're right on time," I manage to reply though once again, he dazzles me and makes it hard to speak.

He gives me an appreciative, sweeping glance. "You look...wow. And you smell wonderful, too."

I pluck at the neckline of my dress nervously. "Thank you. You clean up well yourself."

There's a moment of silence, and I resist the urge to reach for the owl. I keep my voice teasing and hopeful. "Is that for me?"

I know it is since there's no other reason he'd bring it. It's so unexpected and sweet.

Dalton hands it to me. "Yes, it's for you. I saw him in the store, and he looked like he belonged with your other two."

A lustful warmth steals over me, and my pulse quickens with a forbidden longing. This might be the sexiest thing anyone has ever done for me. He brought me a stuffie because he thought I'd like it. Who is this man?

I hold the owl tightly, trying to tame the hunger rushing through my body. Suddenly, a name for the owl hits me, and I grin. "This is Frosty Winks."

Dalton chuckles warmly. "Frosty Winks. That's an excellent name," he replies and gives me an exaggerated wink.

Ha ha, he's a funny guy. I place the owl on the couch with the other two stuffies, taking a moment to arrange them and talk to them in my head. *Okay, guys, here's a new friend. Be nice to each other while I'm gone.* I give each stuffie a pat on the head to show them I love them all equally.

Once I'm satisfied with their placement, I pick up my purse from the coffee table. Turning back to Dalton, conflicting emotions war inside me. I've never been more attracted to a man than I am right now to him. I want to push him onto the couch between my stuffies and fuck his brains out, but I also have an urge to crawl into his lap and snuggle against him.

I tell myself I need to calm down and try to steady my racing pulse, but it's no use. The pounding need inside me blots out all reason, and it's like I have no control over my body. I've been feeling like I don't know who I am anymore, but this person I am right now is another side to myself I've never experienced before. Something has awakened my sexual goddess—and she knows exactly how to get what she wants. He's going to be wrapped around my finger so fast his head is going to spin.

When his eyes meet mine, desire flares in their depths and his voice is husky. "Are you ready to go?"

A current of desire ripples through my body, and my clit throbs. Oh god, the things his deep, rumbling voice is doing to me. How am I going to make it through dinner without throwing myself at him?

Wait, why wait for dinner?

I make a snap decision and drop my purse. "No."

"No? Why not?" Dalton raises an eyebrow, but the heated twinkle in his eyes tells me he knows the score.

The energy coursing through me is incredible, and I'm ready to explore this new side of myself. I slowly kick off my high heels one at a time. "Because I said so."

He gives me a sly and seductive smile while he studies me intently.

Since he's not talking, I continue. "Besides, the whole point of the date is for us to spend some time together, right?"

Dalton finally takes a step forward. "That's the goal," he murmurs, reaching up and brushing his thumb over my lower lip. "So, what did you have in mind?"

I'm wet and throbbing, and he's barely touched me yet. It's a miracle I haven't melted into a puddle.

"You know," I whisper, sounding needy. "I'm hungry for something other than food."

Dalton leans down until his face is mere inches away, and his warm breath ghosts over my cheek. "Tell me what you want, and I'll give it to you."

An intense, primal craving ignites my senses and sends waves of desire coursing through my body. I don't care what he does, I just need him. I stretch upward as my heels lift off the floor and I balance on the balls of my feet so I can slide my arms around his neck, gently pulling on him so he'll meet my lips halfway.

As soon as his mouth is on mine, he takes control. He sweeps me into an earth-shattering kiss, and it feels like fireworks are exploding in my head, sending jolts of pleasure shooting through me. I moan against his mouth, our tongues dueling with passion.

Dalton wraps his arms around me, and I whimper. *Oh yes, touch me everywhere.* With his lips still locked against mine, Dalton's hands trace the contours of my body, coming to a rest on the small of my back. I'm desperate to feel his bare skin against mine, and I'm about ready to push him onto the couch and do whatever it takes to get his cock inside me.

Before I can make my move, Dalton's hands roam down to my ass, squeezing and pulling me tightly against him. I can feel the hardness under his jeans, and the size and thickness are a shock. Well hello, he's obviously not lacking in the dick department. My pussy spasms at the thought of him sliding inside me.

Dalton lifts his head, and his smoldering gaze locks with mine. "I've got an idea. Why don't we skip dinner?"

I can tell he's teasing, and I almost laugh, but I give him a seductive smile instead. "I think that's a brilliant plan, and after I rock your world, just remember whose idea it really was." I poke him in the chest playfully. "You can thank me later."

He answers me with another toe-curling kiss. See, I knew I could get what I wanted.

CHAPTER 7

DALTON

Buying the stuffie for her wasn't planned. I was at the store to pick out flowers when the owl caught my eye. It had glitter on its wings and a cutesy round head. As soon as I picked it up from the shelf, the flowers were forgotten. I knew the owl belonged to her. I should have known we wouldn't make it to dinner as soon as I saw her reaction to it. Her entire demeanor changed, and her skin glowed. It made me want to push her against the wall and ravish her. Olivia is a delightful surprise.

When we first met, she nervously stumbled over her words, and I could tell she thought I was attractive. It was endearing. But when I read her answer on the application about being obedient and flexible, a blast of heat spread through me. The thought of unleashing this hidden side of her piqued a dark curiosity. Then her interview on the radio station changed everything. Hearing her voice and the way she talked about her life in Seattle and going to law school, plus the cute way she described meeting me the day she brought Agnes to the clinic, was another side to her I hadn't seen yet. Now I've got a tempting seductress in my arms, and she's making my head whirl.

Those plump, kissable lips almost made me lose it the moment she opened the door tonight. Her short pink dress exposes her gorgeous legs, and her silky brown hair falls around her shoulders. The best part, though, is her eyes—those sparkling brown eyes stare at me, full of desire and need. I wouldn't have tried to seduce her this quickly, but since she's the one initiating it, I'm going to take what she's offering and make sure she comes so hard she can't think of anything else in the morning.

Capturing her mouth in another passionate kiss, I wrap my arms around her and lift her off her feet. With her petite frame, it's easy to carry her through the cottage. The place is small, and her bedroom is at the end of a short hallway. I'm not surprised to see her room decorated in a pastel rainbow of colors. It fits what I've learned about her so far. I think she's more of a babygirl than a slut.

When we reach her bed, I set her down on her feet. "Babygirl, I want you to strip down and lie on your back in the middle of the bed."

Olivia giggles, the confident seductress melting away as her shyness returns. It's a charming contradiction but not surprising after the way her confidence has shifted throughout the time I've known her. There is something about this vulnerable side of her that draws me in even more, making my heart race with unbridled affection.

She looks down at the floor, and when she doesn't immediately start removing her clothes, I ask, "Did you change your mind?"

"No..." She hesitates a moment before lifting her gaze to meet mine.

I expect to see nervousness, but I'm met with an intense hunger burning in her eyes, and I tremble with anticipation. Like a moth drawn to a flame, I'm mesmerized by her, and the longer we're together, the more this feeling intensifies.

She tosses her head in defiance, her posture straightening as if she's made a decision. "I'm not Babygirl. I'm Kitten."

My cock pulses, and I take a step towards her. I tilt her chin up with my index finger and give her a firm look. "Yes, you are. Now, Kitten, strip for me. I want to see every inch of your delectable body."

With a coy smile, Olivia slowly slides the dress off her shoulders, revealing a pink lace bra. When the dress pools on the floor, I swallow thickly and take a moment to calm my racing heart. Holy fuck, I was right, those legs *are* to die for.

"Now the rest," I order.

Olivia gives a delicate sigh as she reaches behind herself and unhooks her bra. The straps slide down her arms with a rustle, and the lace fabric joins the growing pile on the floor. Her breasts are freed, their pert nipples pebble, begging for attention. She cups them with her palms and pinches her fingers together, rolling the hardened peaks between her fingertips. I can feel my desire building as I imagine sucking and biting on her nipples until she's writhing in ecstasy.

But then I remember myself and bark out a command.

"Stop," I say, my tone more demanding than intended.

Startled, Olivia jumps a little but quickly drops her hands to her sides.

"Did I do something wrong?" she asks softly.

"No," I reply, stepping closer and cupping her breasts with both hands. "You're exquisite."

She moans when my thumbs rub small circles against her nipples. Her cheeks turn pink, and her smile is sexy and adorable. Fuck, I could watch her for hours and not get bored. This woman is a walking contradiction. Shy and submissive one minute, bold and brazen the next.

Keeping one hand cupping her breast, I glide the other down her side, enjoying the smoothness of her soft skin, before hooking my fingers under the waistband of her panties. "Time to get these off."

As soon as they hit the floor, I lean in for a slow, sensuous kiss, our mouths opening in unison, the tips of our tongues swirling around each other's. When she moans and arches against me, my cock presses painfully against the fabric of my pants. Damn, I've got to be inside her.

Pulling back slightly, I stare down at her with a grin. "Get on the bed, Kitten."

Without hesitation, she hops up and settles onto her back and folds her arms above her head.

"Now spread your legs," I instruct and then add, "wide."

Olivia smiles playfully and bends her knees so her feet are flat on the bed and shifts her thighs apart. I wasn't expecting her to be hairless, and I can't tear my eyes away from her glistening pussy. So fucking beautiful.

"Stay just like that," I command and enjoy the sight of her spread out for me. "You've got such a lovely pussy, and I'm going to taste you and make you come. But you're got to promise me something."

"Anything." Her voice is breathless and excited.

"If you need me to stop or take a break, use the word 'red.' Okay?"

Olivia bites her bottom lip and practically moans, "Yes."

That's good enough for now. As I move onto the bed, the mattress sinks down and Olivia's hips rise slightly. I settle between her spread thighs, my face only inches away from her sex, and the aroma of her arousal tantalizes my senses.

I dip my head forward and pause with my mouth right above her pussy, knowing my breath will tickle her. "Kitten?"

"Yes?" she sighs.

I try not to smile from the surge of power rushing through me. This is the part I love.

"Ask for it."

CHAPTER 8

OLIVIA

Holy shit. When he demands I ask for it, a jolt of desire shoots through me, making it impossible to think. When I don't respond after a few moments, Dalton's voice has a playful warning tone.

"Kitten...I desperately want to taste you, but you have to ask for it first."

Oh, god, how does he expect me to talk? I've been fantasizing about fucking Dalton, but the reality is so much better. How can he know exactly how to push all my buttons?

Dalton places soft kisses on my inner thigh, inching closer and closer to my pussy, and whispers. "So sweet."

A tremor runs through me, and my inner muscles spasm. "Please..."

He pauses, his mouth hovering over my pussy again. "Use your words."

Damn him. This is pure torture.

"I need you. Please lick my pussy?" My voice is so weak and raspy, and I'm not sure if I said the words out loud or not.

"Good girl." Dalton hums his praise and gives a long, leisurely lick along the seam of my pussy. My eyes roll back in my head from the exquisite sensation.

My entire body pulses, and a throbbing ache from my pussy makes me squirm, silently begging to be touched. Ohhhh god, I can feel wetness leak out of me, and he uses the tip of his tongue to catch it before pressing his tongue deep inside me.

I moan in bliss as he starts teasing my clit with his tongue. I can't believe this is what I've been missing all these years. No wonder my friends always told me it was great.

Everything he's doing feels sublime, and I buck against his tongue and mouth as the pleasure builds. When he slides two fingers into my channel and curls his fingers to massage the magical spot while sucking on my clit, I almost come unglued. He's determined to draw the experience out, and when I can't take the intensity anymore, he stops, giving me a few moments to recover, and then continues his torment.

Finally, he adds a third finger and begins pumping them harder and faster and sucking on my clit more urgently. A burst of electricity rips through me as I lose myself in a powerful climax. My back arches off the bed as I cry out, and a rush of wetness floods from me.

Dalton groans against my pussy, lapping and sucking, as if he's a starving man. When my breathing calms, he raises his head. "Such a good girl."

My thoughts are a tangled mess. Fuck, what has he done to me? That was the best orgasm I've ever had, but my body craves more.

Dalton climbs out from between my legs and stands up to remove his clothes. Watching him strip is erotic. When he takes his shirt off, he reveals a muscular chest with a light sprinkle of hair. His stomach is just soft enough that it makes my fingers twitch with the desire to explore every inch of him.

He pulls a condom out of his pants pocket and tosses it on the bed next to me, and seeing the square sends a zing through me. His pants and boxers come off quickly. He's got narrow hips and muscular thighs, but it's his cock that fascinates me. His length is a little longer than average, but it's the thickness that's impressive. Would that thing even fit in my mouth? I lick my lips and imagine being on my knees for him. I hope I get the chance to try it soon.

When he joins me on the bed again, he leans on one arm and gently caresses me from my knee to my neck. His fingertips make gentle circles, and I squirm in delight. When he reaches my breasts on his way back down my body, he focuses on my nipple. He rolls it between his fingers before taking the nipple into his mouth.

I moan when he sucks hard. "I need you inside me."

He continues to lick the sensitive bud a few seconds more before chuckling. "I'm not sure you want it enough yet."

What? Of course I do. "Please?"

He affixes his mouth around my nipple again, and I groan and try to pull him on top of me.

He stops sucking, and I almost sigh in relief when he settles between my legs and rolls the condom on before positioning the tip of his cock against my wet slit. He leans over me, kissing me deeply, and the taste of myself on his tongue is wild and exciting.

When his cock presses against my opening, he slides in easily and I moan as I stretch and mold around him. His thickness makes me gasp from pleasure, and when he thrusts in a slow and steady pace, I wrap my arms around his neck and arch against him with every plunge.

"Is this what you want?" he asks, his voice tight with control.

Oh god, every time he talks, it does things to me. I nod, not trusting myself to speak.

"Use your words, Kitten." His voice is soft but still has a commanding edge. He keeps the same pace, relentlessly driving me towards bliss.

"Faster," I whimper, needing him to give me release but loving the delicious tension.

His patience drives me wild, and I appreciate every inch of his cock as he fucks me slowly. The pleasure in my core builds, and each plunge gets me closer to the edge. My toes curl and my thighs tense as his cock sinks as deep as it can go.

I rock my hips, trying to force him to fuck me faster. If he won't speed up, then I will. He doesn't take the hint, keeping his pace steady, and my frenzy drives me to orgasm. Stars explode along the corners of my vision, and I shake as the waves of delight wash over me. I moan long and loud, and he finally speeds up.

"There you go, Kitten," he groans. "Come for me."

My orgasm peaks again, and he grunts as his thrusts grow harder, his hips pistoning so fast I can barely keep up with his movements. I feel like a rag doll being knocked around as he chases his release.

When his thrusts slow and falter, his cock jerks, and he groans as he comes. He shudders before collapsing against me. I'm floating in a haze of joy as we lay tangled together, panting and catching our breaths.

After a few minutes, he raises his head and gives me a tender kiss before slowly pulling out. "I'll be right back."

He rolls off the bed and goes into the bathroom—I'm assuming to remove the condom—and everything clicks into place, like I'm coming back down to earth. Holy shit, that was the best sex of my life. If I was scoring him, that would easily be a 10 out of 10. Two thumbs up. Five stars.

While he's gone, the air is cool against my sweat-dampened skin. I feel surprisingly vulnerable, and I want to snuggle up with him and feel his weight and warmth against me. He returns from the bathroom a few minutes later and crawls back into bed, pulling me into his arms.

I wrap myself around him, and when he feels me shiver, he asks, "Are you cold?"

"I don't know," I confess, not knowing what's wrong with me.

"Poor Kitten. Here, let's get you warmed up." He covers us both with the blanket, then spoons me, draping his arm across my stomach, and pulls me more tightly against him.

Mmm, this is wonderful. His warmth seeps into me, and I sigh with contentment as my trembling stops. I've never felt this connected to anyone after sex, and it's exhilarating. We lie cuddled together in silence, and I try to not think about the future. This is just one date, but after what happened, I want more. I don't want to ruin this marvelous night by asking for anything else.

A text message beeping noise comes from the floor at the end of the bed, and Dalton tenses up. "Shit."

"What's that?" I ask, worried and confused. Why is someone disturbing us?

Dalton sits up, and the blanket falls off him. "Sorry," he mumbles as he gets out of bed and fishes his phone out of his jeans pocket. He reads his text, and I can see the lines on his face harden.

"There's an emergency at the clinic, and I have to go."

"Oh, no," I blurt out, surprised. It's Valentine's Day. Does this happen often?

"Yeah, I'm sorry, but I'm needed."

"Okay," I reply, disappointed but trying to hide it. I don't want to be the asshole who only thinks about themselves when an animal needs help.

He pulls his clothes on and leans over the bed to give me a long kiss. As his tongue swirls with mine, I wish I could tug him back into bed with me. He breaks off the kiss with a groan, and his obvious displeasure at leaving makes me grin.

He looks down at me with regret. "The clinic closes at 5 tomorrow. Do you want to come by at closing, and I'll make this up to you with dinner?"

Holy crap, yes! This isn't a goodbye. My smile widens. "Yes, please."

Relief flashes in his eyes, and he nods. "Good, I'll see you tomorrow."

I call out a soft, "Night," and watch him walk out, feeling a rush of emotions. Damn, his ass looks tasty enough to take a bite out of it.

As the front door shuts behind him and the room is filled with a comfortable silence, a wave of exhaustion overwhelms me. That was the most mind-blowing sex ever, and now I'm completely worn out. After the stress and anxiety of the last couple of weeks, this is exactly what I needed.

Closing my eyes and curling up under the covers, a feeling of happiness steals over me as I replay the last few hours in my mind. My heart fills with hope for the first time since moving to Hazy Cove. Maybe things are looking up after all.

As I drift off to sleep, I wonder if we'll actually go out to dinner tomorrow as a late Valentine's Day date. The sex was so mind-blowing he'll be lucky if I don't jump him the moment I see him.

CHAPTER 9

DALTON

When I crawl into bed at 2 a.m, I groan as my head lands on the pillow. It's never a good night to be called in for an emergency surgery, but interrupting my first date with Olivia was bad timing. I guess I should be happy it didn't happen before we both had orgasms.

Olivia was so sexy, her naked body sprawled on the bed, and the look on her face was a mix of bliss and disappointment. It's nights like tonight that make me wish I weren't the only vet in town, but I still love this job even with being on call during first dates. This also gave me an excuse to invite Olivia out on another date—not that I needed an excuse, but somehow, I feel better this way.

When I'm with her, the rest of the world fades away and she becomes my entire focus. Thoughts of Olivia spread open on her bed seep into my mind. Fuck, she's addictive. I want to see her and be around her again—and not just for sex.

There's something about Olivia that sets her apart from all the women I've dated since my divorce. There's a depth to her that enthralls me, but I wonder if it's too early to tell how deep her layers go. I don't know, but I need to sleep. The clinic opens early, and I can't afford to be distracted by thoughts of our date.

I punch my pillow in frustration, trying to force myself to fall asleep and push aside these conflicting feelings.

I wake up with a sense of anticipation, eager to see Olivia again. Yet as I think about her, an uneasy feeling washes over me and I can't quite pinpoint the cause. I need to figure out what's bugging me so that I can enjoy tonight with her. Hell, what if she's no longer interested after my abrupt departure? What if I've scared her away?

The morning feels never-ending, and I constantly have to dodge questions about my date with Olivia from everyone who comes into the office. It's a slow morning, and I only have four appointments, but with each inquiry, I grow more and more irritated. If I actually did want to pursue something with her, there would be no privacy at all. It's like I'm living in a fishbowl, constantly under scrutiny from all these people who want to know about my personal life.

The only relief comes from Sue, who understands my need for privacy. But even as she avoids asking me questions, I can sense her curiosity lingering in her sidelong glances. It's both a comfort and a frustration knowing that someone is watching out for me but also wanting to keep my secrets hidden.

The only person I want to talk about it with is Travis. He's always got good advice. When I'm finally able to escape to my apartment upstairs and call him at lunchtime, I still haven't worked through my unease.

Travis hoots loudly after hearing what happened. "Wait, you didn't make it to dinner?"

I chuckle and sit on the couch in my living room, hoping to eat quickly and get back to work.

I can practically hear his eyebrows rise over the phone. "Wow, you're not wasting any time."

It's a fair statement. I don't date often, and most of my encounters are one-night stands or at a kink event. This isn't how I would approach a relationship if I was hoping for a love connection. So what does that tell me?

Is Olivia a one-night stand? Last night was amazing, but the more I think about how it went, I don't think Olivia would want to be my submissive—not in how I want one. She talked a good game in her application about being obedient, and the way she went about asking to be called Kitten was fucking adorable, but is she going to want to be spanked and called a dirty little slut? The Olivia I met last night was sweet as candy and all about rainbows and stuffies—not 'I'm going to spank your ass red if you don't obey me'.

"Dalton?"

Oh yeah, Travis. "Sorry," I mumble, realizing I've been silent too long.

Travis sounds reassuring when he responds. "Don't worry about it. You must have a lot on your mind."

I groan softly. "Yeah."

"Listen." He pauses, and I can tell he's choosing his words carefully. "Don't overthink this, man."

Damn him, I hate how well he knows me sometimes. I grunt in agreement, unwilling to say more and give him something to analyze.

When the silence grows, Travis continues. "It's great you two hit it off and had chemistry, but there's no need to rush. Just have fun and see where it goes."

If only that was the case, but damn it, this is a small town and the gossip mill is strong. "We're already the talk of the town. If I don't properly date her, people are going to judge me."

"Ignore the gossip," Travis says with a firmness that almost makes me laugh.

Travis and I have always been able to be brutally honest with each other. So, while the words are blunt and unsympathetic, they aren't mean spirited.

Still, I'm not sure I can ignore everyone gossiping like he thinks I can. "You say that, but—"

Travis cuts me off. "I get it, but what's the big deal? Take the heat and roll with it."

I rub the bridge of my nose and sigh heavily. "Trav, I'm not in the mood for bullshit. Besides, there's nothing to really say. Last night was enjoyable, but I could be worried about nothing. Olivia might plan to come over here and tell me she's not looking for anything more."

Travis is quiet, and the silence hangs heavily between us. When he speaks, he sounds calm but serious. "Well, it's not like you're planning to propose. You could date casually while knowing she's not the person you'll be with forever."

I didn't tell him about my doubts about us having compatible kinks. He's a perceptive little shit. This isn't how I pictured this conversation going, but then again, when does life ever go the way I expect?

I groan and drop my head back onto the couch cushion and close my eyes. "I suppose."

"You've got time," Travis offers. "You really need to relax. She's twenty-four, for Christ's sake. You're ancient. I bet she just wants you to bang her a couple of times."

God, I wish this was a simple thing. It would be easier if the entire town didn't want to know every detail of the date. There's no way they won't continue to ask for regular updates on our status if there's a hint we're together.

"Yeah." I don't sound convincing.

If the situation was different or if we lived somewhere bigger, where no one knew us, I'd be able to take her out and enjoy myself. But in this tiny town, everyone is up in my business and watching my every move. What the fuck was I thinking, entering the contest?

I sigh again, feeling tired and frustrated. "Listen, thanks for the advice, but I need to go."

Travis is the only one who knows I entered the contest to use it as a platform to bring awareness to taking care of pets in cold weather, and talking to Travis clarified a few things. When Olivia gets here, I'm going to tell her this won't work long term. Just one evening with her has me in a tailspin. What would I be like if we were actually dating?

After ending the call with Travis, my appetite is gone, so I head downstairs to the clinic to finish out my afternoon while my thoughts spiral. Shit, I hope she doesn't cry when I tell her I don't want to date. The thought of her looking at me sadly with tears in her eyes makes me sick to my stomach.

CHAPTER 10

OLIVIA

The pink dog collar studded with fake diamonds fits perfectly around my neck. When I look in the bathroom mirror, the diamonds twinkle in the light and make my heart sing with happiness. Thank God I thought to measure my neck before I went to the pet store. How embarrassing would it have been to be trying on collars in the store to figure out my size?

I woke up this morning with a grand plan on how to thrill Dalton, and as soon as my yoga class was over, I headed to the pet store in Ditzel Springs to buy the collar and leash. There's no fucking way I'd buy a blinged-out pink dog collar in Hazy Cove when everyone here knows I have a cat. How does anyone in a small town hide their kinks? Hopefully, no one ever has a reason to check my internet search history.

I already had the leather body harness and black cat ears. I never had time to wear the harness with the asshole ex—we broke up soon after I bought it—and the cat ears are left over from last year's Halloween costume...of course, I went as a cat.

The harness is made of straps that run over my shoulders, down along my sides, and around my breasts. There are buckles that allow me to tighten the straps. There's a thick belt strap that goes around my waist and more straps that circle around my thighs. Just the act of putting it on makes me feel submissive. As I tighten the last buckle, I think of Dalton holding onto the straps while he fucks me and a zing of pleasure through my body makes my nipples harden in anticipation.

I really hope I'm not wrong about Dalton liking this plan.

Now to find an outfit to cover all of this up. Luckily, since it's winter, I won't look out of place in a turtleneck. I match it with a long woolen skirt and ballet flats. A glance in the mirror tells me that no one will realize that all I have on underneath is the body harness and collar. I slip a rolled-up leather leash and cat ears into my purse and smooth my hands down my skirt to relax.

This has the potential to be an amazingly hot encounter or an epic fail. My heart pounds from the uncertainty as I walk out the front door. Time to head to the clinic and hopefully get what I'm craving—his cock in my mouth and a spanking. I don't care in which order.

I arrive at the clinic a few minutes before they close. The parking lot is empty, and the window blinds are closed. That's convenient.

The woman at the front desk is packing up to go home when I enter. "Hey, Olivia," she says brightly, a big smile on her face, and she turns her computer off. "I'm not sure I introduced myself last time. I'm Sue."

"Hey," I reply, smiling back as I try to hide my nervousness.

Sue's demeanor changes, and she cocks her head. "What's wrong?"

Ugh. I guess I didn't fool her. I shake my head and give her a weak smile. "Nothing."

Sue doesn't look convinced. "If you say so. But just so you know, he's a good guy and will be worth the effort."

A warm glow spreads through my mind, and I smile at her. "Thank you."

It's nice to know he treats his employee well enough that she's trying to convince me to stick with him. I can't tell her I'm just here for the kinky sex.

She nods, as if satisfied she said her piece, and stands up, gathering her coat and purse. "He's in his office. He said to send you down there. Everyone else is gone, and I'm locking the door behind me. Have a wonderful night!"

She gives me a wink as she glides out the door, firmly shutting it behind her. As soon as the jingle of the bells on the door fades, I kick off my shoes, shrug off my coat, and remove my turtleneck and skirt. I lay my clothes on the counter with my purse and dig out the leash and cat ears. Once the leash is attached to the collar and the cat ears are perched on my head, I'm ready to find Dalton.

My hair is in a ponytail, and the end swings against my bare shoulders, teasing my sensitive nerve endings. I'm barefoot, and the floor is cold as I head down the hallway. As I get closer to his office, doubts about what I'm doing try to sneak in, but I push them aside. I need to act confident and sexy to pull this off.

His door is open, and I'm surprised to see a lighted candle next to him. His office smells like sandalwood, and it seems to fit the sexy mood I was going for. He's so focused on his laptop that he doesn't notice me. I tap softly on his door. "Sir, your Kitten is here," I announce, giving him my best sultry gaze.

Dalton's head snaps up, and his eyes widen as I sink into a kneeling position. I rest my bare ass on my feet and put one hand on my knee while holding up the end of the leash towards him and lowering my eyes to the floor.

There's a moment of silence that feels like eons. Just as the fear I misjudged the situation creeps in, I hear his chair creak. I lift my eyes slightly, and I see him stand up and come around the desk. My entire body hums alive. Please, please, please, take what I'm offering.

I drop my eyes again, staring at his feet, hoping he likes this display of submission.

He says nothing as he moves in front of me, but my breathing becomes shallow when his fingertips trace the contours of my face and he tips my chin up.

My hand with the end of the leash is still in the air, and when he doesn't take it immediately, I ask, "Does Sir accept my offering?"

Fuck, what if he says no?

Dalton is impossible to read, and the silence is maddening. Finally, he reaches down and takes the end of the leash from my fingers. He gives it a gentle tug. "Stand."

Relief floods through me, and the feeling is quickly replaced with lust. Oh, yes, this is going to be good.

When I rise, he pulls on the leash again, and I feel the collar shift around my neck. "Do you know what you look like?"

My skin prickles with excitement. "Your Kitten, Sir?"

Dalton steps closer and runs his free hand along the edge of the cat ears, trailing his fingers down my neck to my breasts. My nipples are already stiff from desire, and I hold in a moan as he cups my breast.

"You look like a naughty kitten who deserves to be spanked."

Ohhh, fuck yes! I lower my lashes to hide the triumph in my eyes. "Yes, Sir. I've been a *very* bad kitten."

"And do you know why you've been bad?"

Shit, am I supposed to think of something? I love that he's playing along with me. This is going so much better than I expected, but I'm still not sure how to respond, so I say the first thing that pops into my head.

"Because I didn't offer to suck on your cock as soon as I walked in."

As I hear the words come out of my mouth, it feels like my entire body blushes. I can't believe how slutty that sounded. I peek up at him to see how he's taking my confession. One eyebrow is raised, and a smile flirts along the corners of his mouth.

"That's right. You need to learn obedience. So first I'm going to spank you..."

He tweaks my nipple, and a delicious painful twinge heads straight to my clit while he continues. "...Then you're going to apologize for being such a naughty slut before you suck my cock."

I'm on board with everything he's saying, but I stop myself from nodding eagerly. I'm so turned on, my pussy is wet and throbbing, desperate for his attention.

"Yes, Sir."

Dalton pulls the leash, and I step forward, letting him guide me to a corner of the room where there's a large, soft armchair. He points at the chair. "Over the side. Show me that ass."

Holy shit, he's not messing around. Without hesitation, I bend over the side and rest my cheek against the fabric, spreading my legs. A shudder of excitement rolls through me, and wetness drips down my inner thighs. I'm so fucking horny. I've never done anything like this.

I brace myself for the first smack, but instead he runs his hands over the curves of my ass cheeks and hums his approval.

"Such a lovely ass," he murmurs before his voice deepens and he sounds serious. "Remember, use the word 'red' if you need me to pause or stop. Do you understand?"

I murmur agreement and wiggle my ass against his hands.

He gives me a tiny spank that doesn't hurt at all. "My Kitten has to answer me if she wants to play."

My head spins from neediness, and it takes effort to speak clearly. "Yes, 'red' if I want you to stop."

I'm not expecting the immediate sharp spank, and the surprise makes me cry out. When he spanks me again, a warmth spreads through me and my clit pulses. I moan after another smack. It's exhilarating, and I wiggle my ass, desperate for more.

Dalton rubs his hand over the spots he spanked. "Such an eager slut. I bet you're desperate for my cock."

Fuck, I am. I squirm, wishing he was inside me or there was a toy rubbing against my clit. I'm so worked up I could probably come from hearing him talk dirty to me.

Dalton's fingers trace the edge of the leather straps of the harness around my thigh, and I whimper, waiting for him to do something, anything. A finger presses between my ass cheeks, and when his fingertip brushes against my puckered asshole, I jerk and yelp in surprise. His finger is gone before I have time to question whether I want that.

Another spank comes out of nowhere, followed by another, but he doesn't linger, alternating his strikes between the cheeks.

Just when the sting is building, he pauses. "You know you've been a bad girl, don't you?"

Fuck, his voice is like music. "Yes, Sir."

He spanks my pussy, and when I gasp, it quickly turns into a moan when he does it again. Jesus, that feels good.

He does it a third time and my clit throbs. "And why is that?"

Damn, what was the reason? I wrack my brain, and then I remember. "I'm sorry, Sir, I didn't offer to suck your cock when I was on my knees."

"Good girl." Dalton sounds amused, and I feel a jolt of excitement and moan as his fingers run up the length of my pussy and briefly caress my clit.

Dalton makes a hungry noise in the back of his throat, and the sound is a sweet agony. I'm strung tight like a bow, and I wish he would rub my clit some more.

After a long silence, he speaks with authority. "It's time for you to kneel."

Pushing myself off the chair, I sink to the floor, sitting back on my feet. As soon as I'm in place, he walks over to the chair and sits down. He's so damn sexy. He's still wearing his white lab coat, and I can see the outline of his hard cock through his work slacks. I have to fight the urge to climb onto his lap and grind against him. Somehow, I don't think that would get me what I want.

With a tug on the leash, he leans forward and stares at me, and the intensity of his gaze makes me quiver.

"What do you say?"

I blink a couple of times. Does he want me to apologize again? "Sorry, Sir. May your Kitten suck on your cock?"

Dalton studies my face for a moment before leaning back and spreading his knees. "Take my cock out and suck on it."

This feels so damn dirty but also fun, and a rush of power makes my body sing. I'm going to give him the best damn blowjob he's ever had. I reach for the zipper on his pants, and his words stop me.

"Kittens don't have hands."

Oh fuck. I'm so wet and aroused knowing he's going to watch me struggle. I crawl between his legs and use my teeth to try and unbutton his slacks. Shit, this isn't easy. I have to bite the fabric and use my tongue to push the button through the hole. The longer it takes, the fuzzier my head gets, and I can feel myself sinking down into subspace. I'm desperate to get his cock out so I can please him.

It's a huge relief when I finally undo the button, but I still have to get the zipper down. It takes all my dexterity to nuzzle against his pants and get the tiny zipper tab between my teeth. I give it a firm yank, and the zipper opens. *Hah, I did it!*

I meet Dalton's intense gaze, and his eyes are burning with lust. Knowing I've pleased him gives me a rush of satisfaction, but his dick isn't in my mouth. I'm not finished.

His cock is tucked into his boxers, and within a few moments of trying to figure out a way in there with my mouth, I realize it's pointless. Goddamn it. I want his cock. It's like the prize is just out of my reach after I worked so hard for it.

A soft chuckle tells me he knows my dilemma. You know what? Forget this nonsense. I'll make him take it out. I start nibbling on his shaft through the fabric of his boxers, licking him and getting the cotton wet with my saliva.

When he hisses and bucks against my face, I want to do a victory dance, and I redouble my efforts, sucking and nibbling on him, using my teeth and tongue. With a groan, he wraps my ponytail around the hand that's holding the leash and pulls my head up.

With his other hand, he reaches into his boxers, and his cock springs out. It's as thick as I remember, and I'm salivating with the desire to wrap my lips around it.

"Be my good Kitten and get your cream," Dalton orders hoarsely.

Oh, hell yes. I dive in, wrapping my mouth around the tip and moaning as the salty taste of his skin and the tang of his pre-cum hit my taste buds. His cock has thick veins running along the length, and I use my tongue to trace them, enjoying every inch of him.

After I bob my head a few times, I glance up, trying to judge his reaction as I lick the head, tracing around the crown. His jaw is tense, and the cords on his neck stand out.

"Faster," he commands, and lust burns through me like wildfire. The world around me narrows as I focus entirely on his cock and bringing him pleasure. I speed up and take him deep, relaxing my throat. A grunt is the only warning before he pushes me down until my nose is buried into the hair at the base of his cock.

It's all I can do to breathe as he thrusts in and out, keeping me pressed against him as he fucks my throat. It's a glorious amount of roughness, and if I was rubbing my clit right now, I'd probably come with him.

As his thrusts become more urgent, he groans, "Fuck, you're so good at this."

His praise exhilarates me, and I suck harder, desperate to get my reward. When he jerks inside me, his cum sprays the back of my throat, and I swallow. There's so much it's overwhelming, and I can't get it down fast enough.

When he releases my hair, I lick at his softening cock, cleaning him until he shudders and gently pushes me away.

He pulls on the leash. "We're going for a walk."

I grin at him and scoot back so he can stand up and adjust his clothing. I'm trusting that he has no plans to actually take me outside for my walk. He holds onto the end of the leash and blows out the candle on his desk before heading for the door. I lower my hands to the floor so I can crawl behind him. I have no idea where we're going, but it's intoxicating to be on a leash, practically naked, while following him around.

Dalton takes me through the clinic. The cold, hard floor hurts my knees, and the pain brings a hint of humiliation to what I'm doing. I'm willing to be obedient and uncomfortable because he wants me to. He didn't even promise me anything. I'm just this much of a slut.

He opens a door to a staircase leading to an upper level. The wooden stairs bite into my knees, and it's slow going. The stairs open up to his living room, and I get a tiny thrill from realizing I'm in his private domain. This is Dalton's home, his sanctuary, and I'm dying to know how often he brings women home with him. I know nothing about his relationship history, but I'm not going to bring it up right now.

It's homey and rustic, with gleaming wooden floors and dark oak mission-style furniture with green and russet decorations. It looks like Dalton, but it's very much the opposite of me. I like soft, feminine colors and frilly decorations.

"Come, Kitten." He takes a few steps and pulls on the leash.

Oops, I didn't mean to pause. I trail behind him, navigating the hallway until we reach his bedroom. The moment my knees touch the plush area rug at the end of the bed, I want to lay down and roll around on it. This kitten likes to play.

I'm curious about Dalton, so I take a peek at the surroundings. The walls boast a collection of beautiful landscape paintings, and the room is warm and comfortable. Every part of his house and clinic I've seen so far is tidy—an aspect that endears him to me even more.

He has a king-sized bed with a plush navy-blue fleece comforter. No stuffed animals or decorative pillows in sight, which is a mark against him.

When he stops in the middle of the room, I take that as a sign that I can rest in a kneeling position. My eyes follow his movements as he slowly undresses. His muscular arms flex as he removes his shirt, revealing toned shoulders and the softness of his stomach that makes my heart flutter. As he unzips his jeans, I admire the way the denim clings to his powerful thighs and accentuates his strong physique.

His voice is deep and seductive when he speaks. "You know, Kitten, I can't get enough of that mouth, and looking at it makes me want to fuck it again."

Ohhh. I'm in a daze as I think about him fucking my throat and not letting me come. I don't want that...and yet I crave it at the same time. He could toy with me and I'd eventually beg him to edge me. That's how slutty I get.

When he's finished undressing, he stands in front of me and cups my chin. "You've been such a good Kitten, I'm going to reward you. What do you want to do?"

Shit, is this a trick question? What would please him the most? Would telling him how badly I need him inside me please him or does he not care? I stare at his half-erect cock, and my body aches from the desire to feel him sliding between my legs and stretching me as he claims me. Can I admit that?

Licking my lips, I meet his eyes. "Your Kitten needs to be filled."

A glint of desire flashes in his eyes. "Is that what she wants?"

God, he's a tease, but a hot, sexy, dominant tease, and he makes me burn. I'm tempted to tell him he can shove his cock into every hole, and that's not far from the truth, but I want him filling my pussy the most. "Yes, please."

"Then that's what she'll get."

Yes! Dalton pulls me to my feet and leads me to the side of the bed. As he unfastens the leather harness and lets it fall to the floor, his touch is tender. "How did I get so lucky to have such a gorgeous kitten show up at my door?"

I flush, and his fingers lightly travel along my skin, sending goosebumps in their wake. "It was the Valentine's Day contest," I murmur, wishing the moment would last forever.

"That's true." He chuckles. "It's still hard to believe you wanted to be mine."

Mine.

That one word is intoxicating. We both know I'm not his forever, and that's fine. I'll take what he's offering now and hope he wants to continue seeing me. The thought of being his beyond tonight makes me woozy from happiness.

When the harness is off, he guides me to lie on the bed, and I stretch, luxuriating in the softness. Oh god, this is decadent. I might not fully approve of his color scheme, but his mattress and blankets are wonderful.

Dalton leans down and brushes his lips over mine briefly before getting a condom from his nightstand. He puts it on before climbing into bed with me, nudging me onto my side facing away from him. As he presses behind me, I shiver as all my nerve endings respond to his closeness.

When his chest is pressed against my back and his cock rubs against the crack of my ass, he reaches up and plays with one of my nipples.

"So beautiful," he whispers against my neck.

Fuck. His hand on me makes me melt. His fingers drift down, swirling against my skin, and I shudder from pleasure as he slides his hand between my thighs and rubs my swollen clit. I cry out and rock against his hand, wanting more.

He continues his assault, his fingertips circling and rubbing and driving me crazy. Every part of me is a throbbing mess, and I need to come so badly. The pressure builds until I'm right on the edge.

He removes his hand, and I mewl out my displeasure until he pushes my legs forward and the head of his cock prods at my entrance.

He doesn't thrust inside me, and I can't take it anymore. "Please, Sir. Please fuck me."

"Close your eyes," he says as he teases me, the tip of his cock barely pressing against my pussy. "And imagine me waking you up like this every morning, giving my Kitten her pussy full of cum."

My brain blips out at his words, and he sinks his cock inside me, pushing deep until he can't go any farther. He grasps my hip and pulls almost all the way out before thrusting in again. This angle feels wonderful, and it's all I can do not to come immediately.

"That's it," he growls against my ear. "Milk the cum out of me."

Holy shit, he's so dirty, but his words drive me wild. "Yes, Sir," I pant, rocking my hips, trying to take him as deeply as possible, and loving the feeling of him stretching and filling me.

Dalton's strokes speed up, and the sound of flesh slapping and our grunts and cries fill the room. All the muscles in my body are drawn tight, and my heart races with the excitement of knowing he's chasing his own release while also making sure I get mine.

This is the best sex ever. It's like a magic combination of kink, dirty talk, chemistry, and trust, and oh, god, his cock feels wonderful. My orgasm builds, the sensation coming in waves, starting with a tingling in my toes and growing with each stroke until every cell in my body is vibrating with the need for release.

"Sir," I gasp. "May I come?"

"Not yet," he replies as he fucks me faster; his hand is on my hip, tightening.

A whimper escapes, and I'm right on the brink. I'm not going to make it much longer.

Just when I think I'm going to explode, he reaches around me to strum my clit and orders, "Come."

With a loud cry, I jerk as my pussy spasms, and my orgasm rolls over me in waves. I can't breathe, can't speak, can't see. Pleasure consumes me, and all that exists is Dalton and the incredible bliss flowing through my body.

As I'm reeling from the rapture, I feel him thrust into me a couple more times and tense up, moaning loudly. He gives a final shudder, and he stops moving, staying locked inside me.

We lie there in silence, his body wrapped around mine. As his hands trace along my arm, I giggle. I'm sleepy, satiated, and happy.

After a minute or so of us resting together, he shifts and withdraws from me. I make a noise of complaint at the loss, and he responds, "Be right back, Kitten."

When he returns, he has a wet washcloth, and the warmth of it soothes me as he cleans up the sticky mess between my legs. After tossing the cloth in the laundry basket, he gets back into bed and gathers me against him, cradling me in his arms.

As my eyelids drift closed, his voice is soft. "Sleep now."

I need no more encouragement than that. This is the most relaxed and content I've felt since I moved here.

CHAPTER 11

DALTON

Instead of being exhausted like Olivia, I'm energized, and my brain can't stop thinking about the future. Less than twelve hours ago, I thought she was all about lollipops and rainbows, and then she shows up in a harness and collar. Who is this woman and how did I get so lucky?

As her breathing becomes regular, her body relaxes in sleep, and I hold her tighter. When she wakes up, we need to talk. I want this to be more than a fling, and I think we owe it to ourselves to see where this is going. I'll worry about what everyone in town will think another day. Maybe we can sneak around for a bit at first and pretend we're not dating.

The idea of not claiming her publicly as mine doesn't sit well with me, but I don't have to figure everything out tonight. I just know I want more, and I need to find out if she does too.

She sleeps for an hour before stirring in my arms. She rolls over and snuggles closer, her leg wrapping around mine and her nose burrowing against my neck, a small, adorable sigh escaping her. I run my hands along her spine, tracing her shape.

A low moan rises from her, and her hips rock. When she tilts her face up and captures my mouth, a zing of pleasure rushes straight to my dick. My mind is consumed with how exquisite she is and how much I want her again.

Breaking off the kiss, I roll her onto her back and move to get a condom, but before I can reach the nightstand, her fingers wrap around my shaft, giving a few slow strokes.

"What do you want?" I moan.

She stares at me with round eyes, whispering, "More."

Fuck. Me too. I grab the condom and sheath myself and slide on top of her. "Tell me."

As I nuzzle her neck and nibble on the spot under her ear, she threads her fingers through my hair and her breath hitches.

"I want..." She hesitates and trails off, so I stop kissing her and pull back. I look into her eyes and wait, giving her space to say whatever is on her mind. Her cheeks are rosy and her expression is shy, but determined, and her words are whispered. "I want to please you."

"Oh, Kitten. You please me very, very much."

Her blush spreads, and I lower my mouth to hers again as I slide inside her. As soon as her warm tightness clenches around me, I go into a frenzy. Her fingernails claw my shoulders ,and she whimpers and writhes beneath me. It's impossible to go slow, and each moan spurs me on. This isn't going to last long, not with the sounds of her pleasure.

"Oh god," she moans. "Yes."

As I speed up, she wraps her legs around me, locking her ankles behind my back.

"Harder," she begs.

"Fuuuck," I groan as I grab her wrists and pin them over her head. Her eyes go wide as I growl, "Does my Kitten like to be restrained?"

She nods and moans, and I swear she's wetter. Fuck, the idea that she's letting herself be vulnerable and trusting me to give her pleasure is so fucking hot, and I want her more than anything.

When I lean down and capture her mouth again, her kisses are frantic. "Please," she whimpers.

"Come for me, my sweet Kitten."

With a cry, she goes taut, her entire body shuddering as her pussy convulses around my cock. I'm unable to stop myself from coming, and my cock jerks as I follow her over the edge.

I collapse on top of her, and her arms wrap around me, her nails trailing across my shoulders, sending a tingle down my spine. I could fall asleep like this, but a rumbling sound from her stomach reminds me it's been a while since either of us ate. I planned to take her out for Italian food, but that didn't happen, so it's time to make sure my Kitten eats something.

Rolling off her, I head to the bathroom and clean up. When I dispose of the condom and return to the bedroom, she's sitting on the edge of the bed, looking around.

She smiles at me. "You need a stuffie in here."

My heart squeezes with joy. "Oh, yeah?" I'm not a stuffed animal kind of guy, but maybe it's time I become one.

"Uh huh," she nods. "I'll bring one next time."

Next time. That's what I was hoping for.

We order pizza for dinner and snuggle on the couch until it arrives. I set the box on the coffee table, the cheesy aroma already making my stomach grumble.

I flip open the lid and breathe deeply. "I hope you're hungry."

Olivia peers over my shoulder at the loaded pizza. "Starving. That looks yummy."

I grab a slice, the hot cheese stretching as I take a big bite. Olivia laughs, reaching for her own piece.

"We make quite the pair, don't we?" she says. "Lounging around half naked and eating pizza." She's in an oversized t-shirt of mine and is still wearing her collar, while I'm in sweatpants.

I wink at her. "Hey, I'm not complaining. Although, we're missing one thing." I grab the TV remote, surfing through channels until I find a rom-com. "There. Now it's perfect."

Olivia shakes her head, amused. "Do you really watch romantic comedies?"

"I'm a man who likes many things." I really prefer action movies, but something lighter is good for tonight.

She grins. "Okay, Teddy."

"Teddy?"

She leans against me and pokes me in the stomach. "I've decided you're Teddy because you're soft on the inside like a teddy bear."

A gentle buzz in my head makes me feel more content than I've ever been, and my heart melts. I can't resist teasing her, though, and I feign offense.

"I am not! Take that back!"

She pokes the fleshy part of my stomach again to prove her point. "Nope, you're a big ol' teddy bear, and you can't convince me otherwise."

"Oh yeah? I'll show you teddy bear."

I tickle her ribs, and she squeals, nearly dropping her pizza. Her laughter fills the living room. I let up after a minute, not wanting her to choke. Olivia catches her breath, cheeks flushed.

"Truce?" I ask.

"Fine, truce." She leans against me, nibbling her pizza crust.

We settle into easy conversation as the movie plays in the background. Talking to Olivia feels natural, like we've known each other for years rather than days. I learn about her being an only child with a single mother raising her, their frequent trips to Argentina to see her extended family, her passion for hiking, and her secret love of pop music. In return, I tell her about my dream of opening a veterinary clinic since the age of ten, my obsession with action movies, and how I enjoy buying scented candles.

Olivia perks up at that last detail. "Scented candles, huh? Like you collect them, or do you use them?"

I rub the back of my neck, feeling weird about the candles and I don't know why. "Yeah. I use them sometimes. I like aromatherapy and creating moods with different scents. I've easily got over fifty of them in my storage closet."

"That's sort of sweet. Will you show me?"

"Maybe later," I laugh. "Don't want you getting too many ideas about me being a softie."

She smirks. "Too late for that, Teddy."

I roll my eyes in mock exasperation. "You're never going to let that go, are you?"

"Nope, you're now my Teddy," she says, popping the last bite of crust into her mouth.

I like the nickname more than I want to admit, and a comfortable silence settles between us as the movie's credits begin to roll. Olivia rests her head on my shoulder, and I'm content to stay like this all night, holding her in my arms.

After a few minutes, she speaks up softly. "Can I tell you about my ex?"

I tense involuntarily. The fact that he's an ex means something went bad between them. The idea of anyone hurting her makes my blood boil, but I remind myself to be what she needs and not fly off the handle. "Of course. I'm here to listen."

Olivia sits up, hands fidgeting with the hem of her shirt. "His name was Ben. We dated for five years. In the beginning, it was like a fairytale. He doted on me and wanted to be together 24/7. It made me feel so loved and special, but after a while, I realized it wasn't about me. He just wanted someone who would serve him, and I was a willing submissive."

She pauses, eyes downcast. I resist the urge to comfort her, letting her take her time.

"Once I figured that out, I saw how manipulative he was. He controlled everything I did: what I wore, who I saw, how I spent my time. At first I thought he was just really invested in our relationship. But it kept getting worse."

Her voice wavers, and she wraps her arms around herself. "One day, I tried to go out to a movie with a girl I met at school and he lost it. Started screaming about me not respecting him, how I was selfish…"

Tears well in her eyes. Unable to stop myself, I reach over and take her hand, rubbing gentle circles on her palm with my thumb. She grips it like a lifeline.

"He got so angry, and I thought he was going to hit me. We kept fighting and shortly after that, I knew I had to leave." Olivia takes a shaky breath. "My best friend helped me get away, and I ended up here."

She lifts her head, eyes glistening. "So that's my sad story. I'm sorry, you probably think I'm pathetic for staying with him so long—"

"No," I interrupt firmly. "I think you're incredibly strong. Leaving an abusive relationship takes so much courage. I'm amazed by you. Truly."

Fresh tears spill down her cheeks. Before I can react, she throws her arms around me, face pressed into my shoulder. I embrace her tightly, overcome with the need to comfort and protect this remarkable woman.

We stay locked in an embrace until her tears subside. Olivia pulls back, wiping her eyes and giving me a small smile. "Thank you. I don't know why I dumped all that on you, but...it helped to get it out."

I caress her cheek. "You never have to apologize for opening up to me. So you're in Hazy Cove to heal?"

Olivia sighs, and her fingers pluck at the blanket on the couch as she says softly, "I thought so, but I don't feel broken around you."

There's no way for me to hide my grin. That was possibly the best compliment anyone has given me. I pull her closer to me and squeeze her. "I'm glad."

She smiles, some of the light returning to her eyes as she asks, "What about you? Any crazy exes I should know about?"

I hesitate. My marriage didn't end well, and the reasons behind it were complicated. Still, Olivia trusted me with her past. It's only fair that I do the same.

"Well, I was married once. We were high school sweethearts but grew apart." I rub my jaw. "We divorced when I was twenty-seven. She wanted me to be a different kind of partner."

Olivia tilts her head. "What does that mean?"

I clear my throat, choosing my words carefully. ""She wanted me to be a harsher dom than I am. She wanted me to control her all the time. I tried to make her happy, but it wasn't my thing. I'm much more of a...teddy bear, as you put it."

Understanding dawns on Olivia's face. "Ah, I see. Well, she's a dumbass. Who wouldn't want your soft side?" She strokes my stomach with her hand. "You're nice and squishy."

That makes me laugh. Her easy acceptance of me not wanting to always be a dom is a refreshing response.

Olivia snickers. "I take it she didn't want you to buy her stuffed animals?"

I think back to my ex and how she wanted a lot of pain and no softness. "No," I shake my head. "She definitely did not."

I've never met anyone like Olivia, and now that I've had a taste of her, there's no way I'm giving her up. But there is something she and I need to talk about.

"Last night, I didn't take you as the type who enjoyed being spanked."

When her smile turns sultry, my heart rate picks up. She gives a tiny shrug, and her tone is a matter-of-fact, but her words make me burn. "Sometimes, but not always. I like the soft *and* the hard."

How is she so damn perfect? I give her a gentle kiss. "Good to know."

As I brush my thumb along her jaw and down her neck, my fingers drift lower to the edge of the collar. "Then let's take this off you. It's time for soft now."

She laughs, and it's so contagious that I'm laughing with her as I unbuckle the pink collar.

I drop it into her hands and kiss her forehead. "I'm glad it didn't work out with my ex, though. We wouldn't be here right now if it had."

Olivia's cheeks flush beautifully. Our eyes lock, and I know there's nowhere else I'd rather be than right here with this remarkable woman.

She leans in, lips grazing my jawline. "You really are just a big teddy bear."

I smile and kiss down her neck. "Maybe, but I can still show my claws if anyone tries to hurt you again."

"My brave defender."

She traces a figure-eight on my chest, and I capture her mouth in a slow, tender kiss that makes my heart pound. When we finally break apart, Olivia stifles a yawn.

"Someone's ready for a nap," I say gently.

She wrinkles her nose. "Maybe just a short one."

I sweep her effortlessly into my arms, carrying her into the bedroom. Olivia giggles as I tuck her under the covers and slide in beside her. She immediately curls against me, head on my shoulder, as I wrap her in my embrace. Being with her feels amazing, and I never want it to end. I hold her close, and the last thought before I drift off is that the most remarkable woman has come into my life.

The morning comes too soon. Olivia has an early yoga class, and I have to work in the clinic. She dresses in her clothes from yesterday and sneaks out before Sue gets to work. All I can think about is Olivia, and I'm already making plans to spend the evening with her.

I call her at lunch and we make plans to have dinner tonight at her place. She jokes about how we never end up eating. Her bottom might get a soft spanking for that later.

As I'm daydreaming about all the places I want to take her—I bet she'd love the state fair, the farmer's market, and the sandcastle competition in the summer—it hits me. I've fallen in love with her.

It's been a long time since I've felt this way, and it's both scary and exhilarating. How did this happen so fast? Hell, is it possible for this to happen so fast? Jesus, what the fuck is wrong with me? I shouldn't be dating her, and now I think I love her?

I'm stewing about my feelings and wondering if they're wrong when an older guy brings his dog in and asks me how the date went with the young, pretty thing. The way he stresses the word 'young' and waggles his eyebrows makes me realize I need some advice...from my parents.

Since the contest went viral, there was no hiding it from my parents. They know all about it and who I chose. They even listened to our broadcast interviews.

There's a lull in the afternoon, and I close my office door and call them. My mom answers, and I can tell she's on speakerphone, so I assume my dad is close by like usual.

"Mom, Dad, how are you guys?"

"Doing well, son," Dad responds, confirming I was right. "Are you taking good care of the patients?"

"Always," I say with a smile. Dad's the same as ever. He's gruff with a crusty exterior but a softie inside. I come by my soft parts naturally, but I'm lacking his gruffness.

Mom's the opposite. She's soft on the outside, with a rod of steel inside when it's needed. She gushes, "Oh, tell us how the date went with that lovely girl! Are you two going out again?"

Mom's sweet, and it's her opinion about the age difference that I'm worried about. I want to know how she feels about it because she has a better handle on what other women might think.

"Well, actually, I want to see her, but she's younger than me, and I'm concerned it makes a difference. She's 24."

"Yeah," Mom says. "That's quite the difference, but we knew her age from the interviews."

"Oh, right," I reply, trying not to cringe while I wait for her to tell me I need to date someone my own age.

Instead, she surprises me. "Did you have fun?"

Huh, that was a different reaction from what I expected, and it makes me want to tell them more. "Actually, yes. She's really special. I think I'm falling for her."

Dad laughs. "That's great, Son."

I can't contain my curiosity and have to ask. "You're not concerned?"

There's a brief pause before Dad speaks, and when he does, he sounds sincere. "As long as you're happy, I'm not worried—and your mom is nodding her head."

"Dalton," my mom speaks up. "We don't choose the ones we love. As long as she's not pressured or overwhelmed, don't let age stop you from seeing where it goes."

"Thanks Mom. I'll be careful with her."

Little does my mom know, it's been Olivia taking the steps forward in our relationship, so I know it's something we both want. My mom's easy acceptance wipes out any final concerns I had about being older than Olivia. If my parents are fine with it, I can weather anything other people say.

We talk for a few more minutes, and the last thing my mom says before we hang up is, "Bring her to Colorado on your next trip so we can meet her."

I can't stop smiling the rest of the day. The undertone of the call was clear: my parents are excited and happy that I've found a new love interest.

The other person I need to tell is Travis. My phone call to him is quicker than the one to my parents, and it's a funny conversation. His reaction to me telling him I'm going to date Olivia is simple.

With a snort, he says, "Just fuck her and have fun."

That's the plan, but I want him to realize this is more. "No, Trav. I'm falling for her."

"Wow." There's a brief pause and Travis chuckles. "You've got it bad, huh?"

It's true, and now that I'm past the first hurdle, I want everyone to know, including the entire town. But first, I need to tell her.

Travis and I only talk for another minute. After we hang up, I send Sue home early and take a quick shower before going over to Olivia's house. I'm determined that Olivia and I are actually going to eat dinner tonight. We can't always fall into bed together. And if the moment feels right, I'm going to tell her I have deeper feelings for her, but I won't scare her off with the L-word.

CHAPTER 12

OLIVIA

I'm on cloud nine through my yoga class, and the other students can tell. They give me some ribbing and ask the expected questions, but it's not that bad. Everyone likes Dalton, and a couple of the single women are envious but nice about it. How come everyone in this town is so lovely? Even if people had been pissy about my date, I don't think anything can mar my happiness today, but it's great that people are rooting for us.

After showering, I head to the grocery store to pick up supplies for Chicken Alfredo. Cooking isn't my favorite thing in the world, but the thought of making dinner for Dalton tonight brings me more happiness than I expected. But any guy who dates me better enjoy simple meals or lots of take out. It's good that Dalton doesn't seem like the type who expects his woman to stay barefoot, pregnant, and in the kitchen—though I wouldn't mind being barefoot and doing the stuff to get pregnant.

As I shop, I daydream about future babies, and when I realize they all have Dalton's smile, I almost trip. Holding on to the shopping cart stops me from face planting, but my brain buzzes and I'm breathless as the truth sinks in. Holy fuck, I'm already in love with him.

When did this happen? Last night, or was it during the first time we fucked? Or the second or third time? Shit, did it start in the clinic the very first day I met him? I was attracted to him from the beginning, and his dominant streak intrigued me, but it's his kind side and the way he cares about the animals that captured my heart...and maybe Frosty Winks.

Fuck.

This is the best feeling ever…and the worst. No way in hell am I going to tell him I love him. He'll think I'm young and naïve and that there's no way I can love him. If I said it to him and he told me it was simply lust, it would hurt too much. I'll just keep this to myself for a while. There's no harm in that, and I can still imagine him doing all sorts of delicious things to me. There, that's settled.

By the time I get home, I'm flushed from daydreaming about Dalton not using a condom and filling me full of cum every morning. I have enough time to put the groceries away, pick out an outfit, and take a shower before I need to start dinner.

I kick my shoes off and hurry into the kitchen. As soon as the groceries bags are empty, my cell phone rings. It's Sierra. I carry the phone with me to my bedroom, and I'm distracted when I answer. "Yo, what's up?"

Sierra sounds tense. "Go make sure your doors and windows are locked."

A ball of dread immediately lodges itself into my gut. What the fuck? "Why?"

"Ben's in town. Just do it, then we'll talk." Sierra's voice is tight, and I check the bedroom windows before hurrying to the living room.

I'm freaking out. Why is Ben in town, and how did he find me? I'm halfway across the living room when my doorbell rings, and it scares me so badly that I scream.

Fuck, calm down, Olivia. You're not in danger. This is not a horror movie.

I can hear Sierra's frantic talking, but I can't focus on what she's saying. My heart pounds, and as I reach for the deadbolt, the knob turns and the door opens.

Oh. Shit. Fuck. Shit.

Ben is standing on my front porch. He's got a five o'clock shadow and doesn't look like he's slept in days. He looks angry, and his eyes hold a hint of cruelness.

A wave of fear courses through me. All I can do is stare at him, muscles frozen, as a sense of powerlessness makes me feel like a small, trapped animal.

I can't speak, but that doesn't matter because he does, and his voice is sharp and filled with irritation.

"Olivia, we need to talk."

Before I can process what's happening, he grabs my arm and drags me outside, slamming the door behind us.

What the fuck? I'm in shock and can't believe this is happening. "Let me go!"

I try to jerk away and pull my arm from his grip. His expression is menacing, but he drops my arm.

"Don't be like that," he sneers, and when his gaze drifts over me, he narrows his eyes. "Nice outfit."

It takes a moment to remember I'm wearing yoga pants and a t-shirt. The wooden porch is cold, and I'm just wearing socks on my feet. The chill seeping into my bones finally brings me back to my senses.

Unease rolls through me in a black wave, and I shift my gaze from his. "Yeah, well, I would've dressed up if I had known you were coming."

Not.

I can hear Sierra begging me to talk to her, and I lift the phone to my ear. "Hey, Ben's here. I'll call you after he leaves in a few minutes, because he IS leaving."

Fear knots my stomach as I hang up the phone. My thoughts are scattered, and I can tell I'm close to a panic attack.

"Why are you here?" I cross my arms to hide that my hands are shaking.

His nostrils flare. "Where else would I be?"

Umm, literally anywhere else? "Not here on my doorstep scaring me."

Ben rolls his eyes, and bitterness drips from his tongue. "You disappeared without talking to me. When I heard about the stupid radio show date, I came to find you."

Stupid radio show date? STUPID? What an asshole.

Suddenly, the fear is gone, and I can think clearly as anger spirals from the pit of my stomach. How dare he come here, trying to scare me?

I skewer him with a look. "We didn't need to talk. I left you a note explaining that I was leaving."

Ben's eyes widen in disbelief. "Olivia, you're my fiancée—"

"Was," I hiss at him, cutting him off. "I *was* your fiancé. Now you're nothing to me."

His eyes search mine, and when I see them harden, my mind fills with unease. With a shrug, he changes tactics, and says casually, "So, you moved out of our apartment and left a note. And then you came to this shitty little town?"

The more he talks, the more pissed I get. My voice is hard. "Ben, why are you here? Spit it out and then leave."

His hands ball into fists, and he steps towards me. "Olivia..."

I hold up a hand and take a step back. "Stop. No."

He freezes and gives me an incredulous look. "What do you mean, no?"

"Don't come any closer." What does it sound like, jackass? A feeling of dread bubbles up inside me, and the fact he's making me feel this way enrages me.

When he takes another step forward, his eyes darken in anger, and my stomach clenches. Shit, should I make a run for it? He's never physically hurt me, but right now feels different from anything he's done before.

His tone is demanding. "Olivia, we need to talk. I love you."

When he reaches for me again, I almost trip in my hurry to get away. "Ben, stop."

As soon as the words are out of my mouth, he rushes at me and grabs my upper arm, his fingers digging into my flesh as he pulls me towards him and wraps an arm around my waist, holding me close. It feels like a thousand ants are crawling over my skin as I push at him.

His tone turns pleading, as if he's trying to convince me he's not the bad guy. "Baby, you've got this all wrong."

This is so fucked up and terrifying, and I can't do this. I won't do this. I will not allow him to hurt me. Not anymore.

I stop struggling, and I feel deadly calm. "Let. Go."

"Not until we work this out."

Anger flares, and before I can think, I knee his nuts as hard as I can.

He squeaks, and his hold on me loosens. I take the opportunity to reach down and grab his cock and however much of his balls I can get through his slacks, twisting them. Thank God he's always had a small dick.

He cries out and drops his hold on me all together, trying to step back. I follow him, not letting go.

"I said…" I twist a little harder. "You're leaving."

I give him another sharp yank and push him away, watching him stagger backwards. When he reaches for his crotch, a sense of satisfaction floods me.

He crouches with his hands over his junk, tears in his eyes. "Jesus…fuck, Olivia. Are you trying to make me not be able to have kids?"

Staring down at him, I realize he's just a pathetic little man holding his nuts in front of me. I refuse to live in fear of him. I want him gone. Now.

I stand up to my full height and point at the driveway. "You are leaving and not coming back. We're over." I pause, and his shoulders droop before I continue, my voice sounding loud in my ears. "If you ever touch me again, you won't be fathering any children, ever. You won't have balls when I'm done with you."

His eyes widen. "You're fucking psycho. Did you know that? I wouldn't want kids with you, anyway."

A car door slamming closed makes us both glance towards the street. Dalton is striding across the lawn towards us. His jaw is clenched with a murderous expression on his face, but his tone's deceptively mild.

"Are you bothering my girlfriend?"

Dalton's presence and protectiveness overwhelms me, and it's hard not to burst into tears. I swallow and fight to sound steady and confident.

"He was just leaving. Weren't you, Ben?"

Dalton steps close to Ben, crossing his arms and glaring down at him. "Ben has 10 seconds to get into his car if he knows what's good for him."

A look of fear crosses Ben's face as he stands up straight. He's still cradling his injured goods. "Uh, yes. I'm going."

When Ben doesn't move, Dalton points at the driveway and starts counting. "One."

Ben jumps in fright.

"Two."

"I'm going." Ben flinches and holds his crotch tighter, as if he's remembering the pain. "I don't need this crazy bitch in my life, anyway."

Crazy bitch. Fucker. I should kick him in the nuts again and make sure he'll never reproduce. I say nothing and glare at Ben as he speed-walks to his car. Before he gets in, a cop car slows down in front of my cottage and rolls down the window.

"Everything okay? Got a call to check on you."

Oooh, Sierra's wonderful, and she's probably panicking. I remind myself to give her a call once this is over.

Ben dives into his car and starts it, as Dalton calls out to the sheriff. "Yeah, we're fine. The asshole is leaving."

"I'll follow him and make sure he leaves."

I smile my thanks at the sheriff as he rolls up his window and waits for Ben to pull out. When the sheriff drives off and the taillights of Ben's car fade, I start shaking. The adrenaline is making it hard to think. Dalton wraps his arms around me and pulls me against him. A warm feeling settles in my gut.

As he leans down to whisper in my ear, "Are you okay?" tears form in the corners of my eyes.

I nod, not trusting myself to speak, afraid that I'm going to start bawling any second.

"Let's go inside," he murmurs. "It's okay. Everything is fine."

He leads me into the living room and pushes Glacia Pawsicle aside so he can sit down with me in his lap. As he rubs my back, his voice is soothing. I don't know what he's saying, because I'm shaking so hard and all I can think about is how scared I was.

When I finally crack, I can't hold in my sobs. I bury my face against him, and tears leak down my cheeks and onto his shirt. That was so fucking scary.

CHAPTER 13

DALTON

Wrapping my arms around her, I can feel the tension and stress from the last few minutes flowing out of her. It takes all my focus to calm my rage so I can take care of her.

As she clings to me, sobbing, I find myself whispering comforting words into her ear, tenderly rocking back and forth, my hand tracing soothing patterns on her back.

"Kitten, it's okay," I murmur, hoping my presence is helping. "Teddy is here."

Her sobbing intensifies, and the rush of emotions makes her limp in my arms. After a few minutes, I can't help but appreciate how vulnerable and trusting she is in this moment.

When I pulled up to her house and saw her out front with Ben, it sent me into a protective rage. He's lucky I didn't get here earlier, or he really wouldn't have had his nuts when he left.

But Olivia's had a rough time, and all my focus is now on making her feel better. Holding on to her is helping me come down from my high, and I need her just as much as she needs me right now.

After several moments, her tears slow and she's no longer trembling. "I'm sorry."

I gently tilt her head up to meet my gaze and ask, "Are you okay?"

She nods weakly and gives me a faint smile. "I kneed him in the nuts and then twisted them."

A surge of amusement flows through me. "That's because you're my brave Kitten." When another wave of tears threatens to spill, I murmur soothing words again. "Shh," I croon, hoping it helps calm her. "Nothing can hurt you now."

"I'm fine, I swear," she whispers, using my shirt to dry her face. "It must have been Sierra who called the sheriff. I need to thank her."

My heart swells at her courage. "When you do, give her my thanks as well, and tell her that my feisty Kitten kneed someone in the nuts."

Planting a soft kiss on her forehead, I feel her snuggle further into my embrace, her compact frame fitting into my arms as if we were made for each other. The need to keep her safe that washes over me is indescribable.

She giggles softly. "I won't ever twist your nuts...unless you ask for it."

"That's good to know," I laugh, the sound resonating from deep within me.

We lapse into silence, my fingers drawing patterns on her back, as she relaxes against me. Eventually, I whisper into her ear, the words both a promise and a claim. "You're mine."

Her acknowledgment is soft kisses on my neck and a featherlight whisper. "And you're mine."

I hug her close. She is mine, and I'll do anything to keep her safe.

When I brush my lips against hers, she deepens the kiss, moaning and pressing closer against me. I return the kiss, letting her feel all the passion I have for her yet knowing I'm not taking it any further right now. Tonight is for softness and cuddles.

Breaking the kiss off, I cup her cheeks and study her. She's flushed, and my stomach clenches as the seriousness of the situation hits me. "I don't know what I would have done if you'd been hurt."

She replies with a quiet yet strong assurance. "Come to find out, I know how to defend myself."

"Kitten, you've got claws, and they're sexy."

The grin on her face elicits a sense of relief within me. She didn't freeze up in fear, and I'm proud of her for standing up for herself. I make the decision to talk to the sheriff about organizing self-defense classes in the spring. Get someone qualified to train anyone who wants to learn. It might seem like a little thing, but I'll feel better knowing she has some training if she wants it…even if she already knows how to knee someone.

She sighs and rests her head against my shoulder. My heart squeezes, and I want to bundle her up and keep her with me forever.

"Dalton," she whispers, "I love you."

Her declaration leaves me momentarily speechless. I didn't know how badly I needed to hear it. Pulling her closer, I press a light kiss on the top of her head. "I love you too."

She loves me. The sense of completion and belonging that washes over me as our lips meet again is overwhelming, filling every inch of my soul. We have a joint interview with the radio station in a couple of days to talk about our date, and I'm ready to tell the entire town I'm head over heels in love with Olivia. I want everyone to know she's mine.

She suddenly giggles. "So, are you hungry? I vote we order pizza again."

"Okay." I smile at her. "But first you're going to call Sierra and tell her she's awesome, and then we're going to eat and *only* watch a movie. No funny business."

Her nod of agreement and radiant grin tell me she's going to be okay.

"That sounds perfect, Teddy."

Because it is, and Olivia is perfect for me. She's my Kitten, my equal, my partner, and somehow, impossibly, we found love in the air.

EPILOGUE

A Year Later

OLIVIA

Right before closing, I strut into the clinic in a trench coat and four-inch spiked heels. Luckily it's raining today so my coat isn't out of place. What I have on underneath—or rather, what I don't have on underneath—makes my outfit special. I'm naked and I'm ready for Dalton to fuck a baby into me.

As soon as I get inside, Sue smiles and raises her eyebrows at my shoes. "You two have a hot date tonight?"

I smile and shake my head. "Just a surprise for Dalton."

"I'm not asking." Sue winks at me and then goes back to cleaning up her desk.

After the confrontation with Ben a year ago, Dalton and I didn't waste any time planning a future together, and that included a family with lots of kids.

He bought the lot next to the clinic, and we had a house built. He let me decorate it however I wanted. It has lots of rainbows.

We were married a few months ago, and we recently decided it was time to try to get me pregnant. The decision brought out a magnificent dirty-talking side of Dalton, and I've been a wet mess all day plotting out my surprise for him tonight.

Once Sue leaves, locking the door behind her, I make sure all the blinds are closed before shrugging off my coat and pulling the cat ears out of my purse. As I adjust them on my head, I think back on how far we've come since I first showed up at his office with the pink collar. A lot has changed, and yet we're still the same—I'm his Kitten and he's my Teddy. But tonight, I don't need Teddy. I need my Dom.

I keep my high heels on, and they click loudly on the hard floor as I slink towards Dalton's office. He's sitting at his desk, and he glances up as I approach.

When he sees me, there's a moment of surprise reflected in his eyes, and I hold in my grin. That's right, my man didn't expect me to walk in naked.

I lean against the door, striking a seductive pose. "I've come for my breeding."

He recovers quickly and gives me a look of pure heat. As he stands, his eye rove up and down my body, his gaze hungry and filled with lust.

"Come with me, Kitten. You look like you need a thorough examination."

Desire simmers in my core as I follow him to the closest exam room. He's bent me over every surface of the clinic in the last year. It never gets old.

He pauses next to the metal table, and as I approach him, he grins. "You've been a horny, naughty girl, haven't you?"

"Yes, Sir," I say breathlessly, loving the way he looks at me like I'm his entire world.

When I reach him, he pulls me into his arms. His lips capture mine, his tongue delving into my mouth and his kiss possessive. He grips my ass and pulls me closer, and I whimper when I can feel the hardness under his slacks.

When we break apart, he turns me around and slaps my ass.

"Bend over," he commands. "Put your hands on the table, ass in the air."

Mmm, yes, Sir. I quickly follow his orders, putting my palms flat on his desk, bending forward, sticking my butt out. I spread my legs, showing him everything, as excitement courses through me.

I flash a wicked smile at him over my shoulder and wiggle my ass at him. When his hand lands on my butt, a delicious thrill runs through me. I can't believe this is real life, and sometimes I have to pinch myself that I'm married to the most wonderful man in the world.

Another swat on my bottom, and I cry out from the delicious pain. I didn't come here to get spanked, but I'm not complaining.

I hear the sounds of his clothing rustling as he undoes his zipper. "Time to breed my sweet Kitten."

His words send a flood of wetness between my legs. There is nothing sexier than feeling him blow his load deep inside me. I love how I can still feel it long after we're done making love.

Suddenly, his hands are on my hips and his cock probes the entrance to my pussy. When he teases me with just the tip, his voice is husky. "This pussy belongs to me, and I'm going to fill it so full of cum it's going to drip out of you for days."

Fuuuck. I love it when he talks dirty like this. I moan, wanting more.

As he pushes inside, stretching me, I moan out a long, "Yesssss."

He begins to pound into me. "You're such a desperate little slut for my cum."

Yes. Fuck yes. That's exactly what I am and his dirty talk turns me on.

"Please, Sir. Fill me up. Breed me." I arch my back and stick my ass up higher.

His fingers dig into my flesh, and his cock stretches me wider with each thrust. At a sharp smack on my ass, I cry out and the bite of pain sends a jolt of arousal straight to my clit. Each stroke causes the tip of his cock to rub against a magical spot, and I'm already on the brink of coming.

"Kitten," he growls. "If you want my cum, you're going to have to beg for it."

Shit. Fuck. Please. Now. A million thoughts fill my head, but nothing comes out. I'm lost in a haze of pleasure and overwhelmed. When his fingers find my clit, I scream, my body no longer under my control. All I can do is let the orgasm roll through me as the bliss skyrockets me higher and higher.

He continues hammering into me, the table banging against the wall with his frantic pace. When he can tell I've come down from my orgasm, he laughs. "Now, my sexy little slut, you better beg for it or I'll pull out and come all over this pretty ass."

What? No, he can't do that! The rational part of my brain knows he wouldn't actually do that, but I'm too far gone to do anything but beg. "Nooo, please. I need it inside me. Breed me, please?"

He thrusts harder, making the table creak. "You can do better than that."

My head spins, and I try to remember what it was I was supposed to do. Oh right, beg. A rush of words comes out, and I don't know what I'm saying.

"Please, please, please, Sir, I need your cum." I take a breath and continue. "Breed me and put a baby in me. I want to feel you explode inside me, filling me, coating me with your seed."

He gives a sharp thrust, and I can feel his cock pulsing. He groans, "Time to fill my goddess with my cum."

I grip the edge of the table and moan as he gives one final hard whack and holds himself still. His cock jerks and throbs, and he cries out as he pumps me full. The sensation of his warm cum shoots me over the edge again, and I shudder as waves of pleasure run up and down my body. I writhe under him, shuddering with delight.

I don't know how long my orgasm lasts, but as soon as I come down, his cock slides out of me and he helps me stand. There's an emptiness, and the sudden coolness, a reminder that my pussy is no longer stuffed, but the trickle of wetness as his cum leaks out of me makes me smile. Oh yeah...this is the good part.

He sits down in the closest chair and pulls me into his lap, kissing me deeply. When we stop kissing, he adjusts my cat ears and smiles at me. "I love my sexy Kitten."

"Meow," I purr at him and return his smile, snuggling in this warmth.

Someday soon I'll hopefully be his pregnant Kitten. It's a good thing he wants a large family, because once I found out how he loves to talk filthy to me while breeding me...he's going to be one busy man knocking me up until the end of time.

I don't want him to ever stop breeding his Kitten.
The End

LOOK FOR THE ENTIRE SERIES!

First in the series, Spanking & Sprinkles, by Reba Bale.

A grouch who's really an alpha cinnamon roll, a sunshine who's really a brat, and a Valentine's Day date they'll never forget...

Maddie

When you're short and curvy and run a cupcake shop, people naturally think you're sweet. Sweet – I hate the word! I can play the part, but my friends know the real me: she's a little quirky, has the sense of humor of a pre-teen boy, and swears like a sailor.

After a string of dating disasters, two of my regular customers encourage me to sign up for the local radio station's Valentine's Day matchmaking contest. I'm about to tell them no, but then I see Hazy Cove's tattooed bad boy is one of the contestants. After I pick my jaw up off the floor, I know I have to apply. Everyone in town thinks he's untouchable, but I have a few tricks up my sleeve...

Buck

When you're tall and muscled and run a tattoo shop, people naturally think you're tough. And it's true – except where my grandmother is concerned. When she decides to sign me up for some stupid dating contest, I don't have the balls to tell her no, which is how I find myself clicking through applications from the women crazy enough to enter to win a date with me.

When I see the sweet little gal who runs the cupcake shop, I know she's the one I should pick. All she'll need to do is spend a few hours with me and she'll run screaming from my dominant desires before she even gets a glimpse at my toy collection. I'll be off the hook with Nana Daisy and maybe I'll get some free cupcakes out of the deal.

Turns out my sweet little baker is submissive in all the best ways – and that smart mouth of hers is giving me all kinds of ideas...

Check out all the books in the Love is in the Air series at your favorite retailer.

Book 1 – Spanking & Sprinkles by Reba Bale

Book 2 – Blindfolds & Butterflies by Meg Becker

Book 3 – Restraints & Rebounds by Eliza Black

Book 4 – Praise & Paperbacks by Kristin Lance

Book 5 – Kittens & Collars by April Cross

About April Cross

April Cross (also Lacey Cross)

Writer of spicy stories... okay, I'll be honest, most of my stuff is ghost pepper spicy. I started writing wife sharing stories before branching out to longer romantic erotica series and stories. I write power play stories with guys who demand to be in control. If you like short and super spicy wife sharing stories, check out my Lacey Cross books.

Website:

https://april-cross.com/